MW01610972

SPRING IN SWEETWATER COUNTY

CIARA KNIGHT

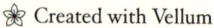 Created with Vellum

Chapter One

JAMES BENJAMIN CLIMBED out of the car, scanning his childhood home. Gravel crunched beneath his feet, the only other noise in the quiet countryside besides Eric Gaylord's idling vehicle. He clutched the door, steadying himself as he took in the peeling paint, broken shutters, and overgrown front lawn. Only the spring floral scent and specks of purple wild flowers in the pasture looked familiar.

He glanced at Eric, who cut the engine, hopped out and leaned against the hood. "It functioned as a boarding house for a while when the college was built, but now we have to chase vagrants away. That's why the county's pushed to either fix up the home and sell it, or tear it down."

James' gut clenched tight. *Tear it down?* His mother had given everything up to be with him when he needed someone. She'd abandoned the home and town she always loved without barely a word. Looking at it now, he realized how much she truly sacrificed for him. "My uncle. Did he not care for the house?"

"I'm afraid not." Eric sighed and shook his head. "You don't have to spend the night here. Why don't you stay with me? You can search the old house for your proof of life papers in the morning."

James only shook his head. "After all these years, I once again have to prove I'm alive instead of buried somewhere back in Nam." He sighed. "I'll let you know when I find the documentation so we can start the process of selling the house." He grabbed his duffle from the trunk of Eric's car, stepped over several broken boards and climbed the few steps to a past life. Pausing on the front porch, he turned to watch Eric drive off before facing his demons.

The door stood ajar, the lock long since broken. He shoved it open and ducked under the strings of cobwebs.

For months, while living in a Vietcong prison camp, he had dreamed of returning home, marrying Judy and living happily ever after in this house. His parents had talked about downsizing and building a cottage on the other side of the property. But none of that was to happen. He hadn't stepped foot in the house since *that* night.

The horrible night when he'd almost strangled his mother to death.

Stumbling, he kicked an old picture that had fallen from a wall. He lifted it and brushed the gunk off with his fingertips. The old family photo, with his parents, Judy, and himself on prom night, felt like a thousand pounds pressing down on his legs. He dropped to his knees, clutching the broken frame to his chest. It had been so many years.

It felt like a lifetime ago. "How could I have failed so many? I should've been stronger."

For the first time since his mother died, he wept.

"I CAN'T BELIEVE HE'S ALIVE." JUDY GAYLORD GRAZED HER finger over the creased photo of her first love, James Benjamin.

The room moved under her feet and she clutched the antique table with her spare hand.

Lisa wrapped a loving arm around Judy's shoulders and guided her to a chair near the back of their antique store. "Here, sit."

How many times had Judy imagined crawling into the picture and cuddling next to James? She pressed the image of the dark-haired, blue-eyed love of her life to her heart, trying to still the thrashing against her sternum. "They say time heals all wounds, but I think they're only mended with thin sutures." She looked down at the photo once more. "And for the second time in my life, this man has left a gaping hole in my heart."

Lisa sat beside her and took her hands. The girl had fast become her best friend and she dared to hope her daughter-in-law, hopefully before her baby arrived. "I'm here. The way you've always been there for me. It's okay, just take a deep breath." Lisa bowed her head. "I didn't know if I should tell you."

"Of course you should," Judy snapped. Yet one breath later, she realized ignorance was bliss. "I trust my son, but how did he find out James is alive?"

Lisa took a long breath. "Eric waited until he was sure. Then he flew to Miami and met with James. I'd never put you through this if I wasn't positive."

Judy stared at the younger woman blankly for a moment. "Then how?"

Lisa flicked wayward lint from the cloth placemat in front of her. "The county retained Eric to contact the next of kin for the Benjamin estate prior to it going to auction. When he dug deep enough, he discovered your husband's cousin was alive. That he'd been living in Miami since 1974."

Judy gasped. "1974? Are you sure? No, it can't be him. James was captured and killed during Vietnam. It's not possible. There's a mistake. If he was alive, I would have known. I wouldn't have…"

"You wouldn't have been with Michael. It's okay." Lisa squeezed her hand. "Eric knows."

"I didn't mean—Oh, I don't know what I mean. I'm all twisted up inside. I loved his father, you know that. Michael gave me the greatest joy in my life. Eric."

"And he knows all about it. Eric doesn't begrudge you for marrying his father, and he knows you always treated Michael well and loved him." Lisa leaned forward. "But Michael's gone now and the man you once loved is alive."

"There are so many questions, I don't know where to start." Judy took a long, deep breath. "Why is he returning now?"

Lisa leaned back again then rested a hand on her bulging belly. "The documentation that proves James returned from Vietnam alive was destroyed during a flood in Nashville. Apparently, he doesn't have a copy, but believes his mother did, so he's come here to search her things to see if he can find it. If he finds the documentation, it will expedite the procedure to transfer the house into his name so he can sell it. Eric went down to nudge him, explaining that it would be a lengthy process to re-file."

"So, that's the reason he's come home." Judy fought the disappointment welling up in her chest, but it nearly choked her.

Lisa rose from the chair, running her hands along her lower back. "I brewed tea this morning. I'll go get it."

"No, sit." Judy shot up, nervous energy pushing her to move. "You need to take it easy. We don't want that baby coming early."

"Fine, but when you return I need to tell you more about Dr. Benjamin."

"Doctor?" Judy chuckled. "I always knew that man was full of greatness, but doctor?" She rested her fingertips on top of the table for balance and twisted left then right, scanning the thriving shop she'd opened with Lisa only a few months earlier. She'd found success, too. Would James be proud of her? She shook the thought from her head.

"What are you thinking?" Lisa smiled up at her, her slightly puffy pregnancy cheeks glistening under the muted light of the chandelier. "I'm here. Talk to me."

"It's silly."

"No, silly is me eight months pregnant, hoping to marry your son after only knowing him a few months. Crazy is you and me starting this business without even meeting except over internet and phone. Crazy is you loving me despite the fact I'm carrying my ex-fiancé's child."

"Yeah, that is crazy. Beautiful and amazing, but crazy," Judy teased, trying to avoid answering her question. "You know how I feel about you. I'm proud of how brave you are and I can't wait to see you marry my Eric."

"Judy Gaylord, I know you. Stop trying to change the subject. Now, spill it." Lisa's brow narrowed with mock agitation.

"I was wondering if he'd be proud of me. I mean, he's a doctor. I opened an antique store, but that was only recently."

"Of course he'd be proud of you. Not just for this store, but for the amazing, loving, giving, and capable woman you are."

Judy waved her sentiments away. "Please. This is stupid. The man is dead. And if he lived in Miami all these years and didn't tell me he was alive, I'll kill him so it won't matter anyway."

"You don't mean that." Lisa rubbed her protruding belly. "You're just scared."

Judy humphed and marched to the kitchen. That man had some serious nerve showing up here after all these years. After what he'd put her through. She retrieved the rose china set she'd acquired from a garage sale at the Benjamins' farm twenty years ago. The set had belonged to his grandmother. A treasure to the woman she once loved and thought would be family, before she betrayed them all. She carried the tray back to where Lisa sat. "If he's been in Miami he doesn't want to be here, which means he doesn't want to see me." She waved her hand at Lisa before the girl could protest. "Which is fine. I can accept that."

Lisa huffed.

"What?" Judy asked, narrowing her gaze.

"Please. You've never let anything rest a day in your life. You'll never be satisfied, not without some answers. If you don't want to face him, then tell me what you want to know and I'll ask him."

Judy poured bronze liquid into the teacups. "I know what happened."

Lisa dropped a sugar cube into her tea and stirred, swirling a hint of mint into the air. "You need to stop beating yourself up about what happened. I know you were hurting. It was an unimaginable loss. James will understand."

"Will he? I don't know. You weren't there. The way it all happened, I mean. It was a disaster, I hurt so many people. I ran off a second after hearing the news about James' death, straight into the arms of his cousin. I got pregnant with Eric." She sighed. "Of course he hates me, just like his mother did."

Lisa's phone buzzed and she glanced at the display. "I guess it's time for you to find out. Eric just dropped him off at the farm."

A bolt of anxiety shot through her. How could she face him? What would he say? Did he have a happy life? All the questions muddled together in her head, but only one slipped from her mouth. The one she'd been holding in since the second Lisa told her James Benjamin lived. "Is he married?"

Lisa's mouth quirked up on one side. "No. From what I understand, he never married."

Judy forced her out of control nerves to calm down. Lisa was right, she'd never be able to settle without finding out the truth. It had been over forty years, and she wasn't going to wait another minute. "Will you be okay until Eric returns?"

Lisa's smile grew into a teeth-baring grin. "Of course. You go make that man explain himself."

"Oh, don't worry. I will."

Chapter Two

AN EVENING CHILL swept through the house from a broken window, straight to James' bones. He'd never been in his childhood home when there wasn't life surrounding him. Boisterous laughter, his mother's singing and father's tinkering with household projects once filled this entryway, echoing up the stairs to his room. Even though he'd been an only child, they always hosted family and friends. Christmas, Easter, and Fourth of July were massive events that half the town attended. Their long drive would be filled with cars and fireworks would ignite over the small lake out back until the early morning hours.

Had the house sat silent since 1971? Did his family die with him inside that cage in Vietnam?

Still kneeling on the dusty floor, he fisted his hands tighter around the framed photo to stop their trembling. Wiping the back of his sleeve across his eyes and nose, he shoved up from the floor and gently placed the old family photo in its original resting place, leaning against the wall.

Enough of this. He'd learned a long time ago feeling sorry for yourself, grieving for a past life, led nowhere. Pushing his shoulders back, he marched up the stairs. If any documentation remained, it would be up in the attic.

He gripped the railing and marched up the steps, determined to find the paperwork and leave town before someone noticed him. Each step creaked with memories. The third plank gave way and his foot slipped through the hole, the splintered wood ripping his trousers and slicing his leg. A thick splinter impaled his lower calf as blood oozed from around the punctured skin. Leaning against the wall, he lifted his leg, breaking the splinter off. With a quick inhale and slow exhale, he crouched and pulled the wood from his leg, before collapsing on the step above.

He inspected the droplets of blood staining the half-painted, grungy step. The pools of crimson liquid, mixed with dirt, transported him back to the night he'd struggled for over forty years to forget.

Heat the temperature of hell, wet dirt and the smell of death suffocated him. He needed a break. A chance to breathe and walk, instead of remaining crouched in a foxhole for eternity.

"Mason, latrine break. Cover."

Mason nodded and shot up, with his M16 aimed at the thick vegetation on either side. The home of predators...deadly snakes, poisonous arachnids, and the Vietcong.

Plunging his boot into the muck, he slid on his belly to the surface. With a trained eye, he crawled past another foxhole several clicks away then crouched, disregarding the stench of the latrine.

Droplets of dew slid down a long leaf, reminding him of the early hour. Wet everywhere, his fatigues, plants, dirt. He dreamed of a life back in Sweetwater County, dry and with Judy in his arms.

He stretched, alleviating the tension in his back and shoulders. It had been days since the last conflict, but danger still rested anywhere at anytime. The Vietcong were artists at stealth approach. It was their home, and he couldn't help but feel like he didn't belong.

He sat on a rock and took a swig from his canteen, trying to fill his lungs with the hope of freedom. With a yawn, he slid the picture of Judy from his pocket and gazed at her beauty. If he didn't hold it in his hands, he wouldn't believe anything but suffering, danger, and ugliness remained in the world. One look at her auburn hair and bright eyes saved his heart from desperation. It wouldn't be much longer before he'd be home. That was his mantra. Not much longer and I'll have my life, my dream.

Snaps in the distance and the flight of birds startled him back to reality. He shoved the picture in his pocket then clutched his gun to his chest and raced back to the line. Heart pumping loudly in his ears, sweat dripping down into his eyes, he slid through the muck back to the foxhole then scanned the area. No sign of life. Not even a rodent or bug. The eerie silence made the hair stand all over his body. They were here. The Vietcong. Swallowing hard, he army-crawled to the first foxhole, choking back a scream. Mason? Jackson?

He didn't want to look, he didn't want to know. Were all his friends murdered while he sat dazing at a photo of his love? Did he fail them?

His hands shook so much, the clip rattled against his weapon. With one last shove, he fell into the foxhole, gun ready to fire.

Dead.

All of them.

Killed with a silent blade across their throats.

❧

JUDY GRASPED THE OLD WOODEN RAILING AND LOOKED UPWARD in disbelief. She'd known the farmhouse had passed through several tenants, but she could never bear to turn down that long drive and face the home she longed to live in since she fell in love with James.

Scanning the front porch before her, she spotted a large footprint leading to the ajar front door. Inside, the house stood silent and dark. It had all been a mistake. James was dead...he had to be.

A deep howl, like that of a dying animal, shattered the evening quiet. "No! Ahh!"

She stumbled back down two steps. Not an animal, a man.

James? Something was wrong. She snatched her pepper spray from her purse and charged through the door. She broke through cobwebs, stumbled over an old overturned chair and fell against the entry way wall.

James. He sat on the stairs only a few feet away, holding his bleeding leg. She shuffled closer and caught his gaze. His eyes were wide and wild, like a caged animal. Not the soft silver eyes of the man she once loved.

"James?"

His head snapped in all directions at the sound, hands raised in defense.

Judy nudged closer then dropped to her knees. "It's okay." Her fingers released the canister of pepper spray and it rolled across the wood floor. The noise drew his gaze then his head snapped back to her.

"Judy?"

"Yes. It's me." She reached out, but he cowered away like a wounded dog. Noticing the bloody splinter and gaping hole in the step below him, she said, "It's okay, I just want to help." She indicated his leg with a tilt of her head. "It seems this old house tried to swallow you up," she teased, hoping to calm him. "You're sweating. You okay?"

James averted his gaze and shifted his leg away from her outstretched fingers. "You shouldn't be here."

She froze, his words slashing through her like a Tennessee tornado.

He rubbed his forehead. "I-I didn't...hurt you, did I?"

"No." She hesitated then tried again, reaching out to lift his pant leg and inspect the damage to his calf. "You didn't hurt me, but it looks like you did a number on yourself."

James scooted backward, pressing his body against the wall behind him as if her touch would send him straight to hell. "I'll be fine. Go. Leave."

Does he hate me that much? She wanted to run from the house and never see those eyes look at her with disappointment and anger, but she couldn't leave him like this.

Judy tugged the scarf from her neck and wrapped it around his calf. Her fingers brushed his leg and only then, feeling the heat of his skin, did she accept he was real. She swallowed a gasp then busied herself with the makeshift bandage. His calf tensed at her contact, but she ignored it and secured the scarf with a knot. "An Eagle Scout taught me that." She smiled then scooted to the lower step.

Grabbing her handbag from where it had fallen sideways, she scooped the contents spread across his floor back inside. "I should drive you to the hospital."

"No. The cut is deep, but small. Just need to wash and bandage it. I'll be fine. Go." James straightened and pulled himself upright, puffing out his chest. He'd grown into a strong man. His shoulders and arms had filled out, his hair now silver, matching his eyes. He was the same man, yet different.

"You were gone all these years. Presumed dead." Judy swallowed a soft cry. "Now, you return."

He ran a hand through his shiny flattop. "I didn't...I couldn't."

She shoved from the floor and stood a few feet away. Even in the dim light, she made out the familiar, long, dark lashes accentuating his silver eyes, but the crease on his forehead was new. Did he still have knee-melting dimples when he smiled?

They stood there in the dingy, old house, staring at each other. Only the chirping outside and her rapid pulse hammering in her ears made a sound.

"Why?" she asked finally.

James opened his mouth but shut it again without a word. He wobbled then clutched the handrail to steady himself. "You need to go."

Judy couldn't move. All she could do was stare at the man before her, former captain of every sports team at Creekside High

School, the romantic gentle giant she'd once loved with all her heart.

"I said you need to leave." He jutted out his chin and stared past her, over her head, though he couldn't hide the fact his hands still shook uncontrollably.

She wanted to scream at him. Call him an idiot—a selfish, lying animal that didn't deserve her guilt. But in the next instant, she wanted to beg his forgiveness. For once she couldn't speak. Not even to say she was glad he was alive, or threaten to kill him for making her believe he's been dead all these years.

Shuffling to the front door, she finally choked out, "I'm sorry." She leaned her head against the doorframe, fighting her willful mind to stay and confront him, but their emotions were high and as much as she wanted to help him with his distress, she knew she'd only provoke him more.

Silence lingered until he finally whispered, "I'm sorry, too."

She spun around. Her hands on her hips, she took two steps toward him. "You want me to leave, fine. I'll go, but on one condition."

He sighed. "What's that?"

"You don't leave Sweetwater County without answering my questions first." She swore she saw a hint of a grin on his lips before he cleared his throat and that distant look replaced the glimmer of happiness.

"I promise."

Chapter Three

Judy shuffled into the coffee shop and inhaled the rich aromas of breakfast and freshly brewed heaven. Cinnamon and coffee grounds awakened her senses, as did the sight of the espresso machines sending steam into the air. She hung her jacket on the rack then froze.

Cathy Mitchell sat a few feet away, and knowing that woman, she'd corner Judy the first chance she got about the estate sale. If anyone knew about James Benjamin, it was Cathy.

Cathy hadn't spotted her yet, and Judy could always make a cup of tea when she got to the store. Reaching up to retrieve her jacket, she heard Cathy's boisterous voice boom through the small shop.

"Rose Burton, that's bull hockey. Now, you know I don't weigh no hundred and twenty-five pounds. I haven't seen that number in decades."

"Mrs. Mitchell, it's an online dating profile. Trust me, everyone fibs." Rose smiled warmly as she typed away on her laptop.

Online dating profile? Cathy Mitchell? Judy couldn't possibly pass up hearing about this.

"We shouldn't lie," Cathy said.

Rose flipped her long hair back over her shoulder. The girl had to be around sixteen or seventeen. How'd she get mixed up with Cathy Mitchell? "Don't worry. I'll get you into my gym. Matt, my trainer, is sick. He'll have you looking like you are twenty-five again in no time."

Cathy giggled like a schoolgirl. "Well, perhaps just write *young at heart* and *as shapely as when I was twenty-five*. I don't want to work with a trainer who's ill. I'm too old to get the flu, it'd kill me."

Rose chuckled and hit a key dramatically with her pointer finger. "And you're live."

Judy smiled. A good man could soften Cathy's edges. Perhaps she'd even be the girl Judy once knew in high school, before everything changed.

Cathy fanned her face with her napkin. "I guess if I watch what I eat and exercise a little, I could make that mark by the time anyone replied to my profile thingy."

Ding.

"What's that?"

Rose giggled again and shifted in her chair. "Someone contacted you based on your profile."

Judy shuffled closer then leaned over Cathy's shoulder. "Guess you best get to the gym."

"Oh—what? You? Humph. Now you listen here, Judy Gaylord. You just stop being so high and mighty, because we both know you're facing your own scary future." Cathy turned back to Rose, who had already closed her laptop and was shoving it in a school backpack.

"You can check your profile when you get home," Rose said, standing up. "I gotta bolt if I'm gonna make first period."

"Thanks, sugar. You're such a sweet girl. Much sweeter than most." Cathy shot a sideways glance at Judy.

Judy longed for her best friend from high school, the one who made everything better. The only person in this town that knew James as well as she did, but Cathy wasn't that person anymore. Instead, she marched to the register.

"Hi, Mrs. Gaylord. Your usual?" Marcus Vega asked from behind the counter.

Judy pulled her wallet from her purse and handed him her credit card. "Yes, please."

"London Fog," he yelled back then took her card. "You okay, Mrs. G? Your hands are shaking."

She smiled and nodded, afraid her voice would crack if she tried to speak. Luckily, Rose sauntered up to the counter.

"Bye, Marcus. I'll see you after school."

His eyes lit up like Fourth of July fireworks at the Sweetwater County picnic. "Look forward to it," he said, his Hispanic accent more pronounced and suave than how he'd spoken to Judy moments before.

Rose paraded off, flipping her hair back once more. Had Judy ever acted like that around James? God, but it was so long ago.

"Mrs. G, your credit card. You sure you're alright?" Marcus asked.

"Yes, sorry." Judy slid to the side as Cathy waltzed up to place an order. Fifty questions and five changes to her order later, Marcus finally had her order.

Judy danced between feet, willing the barista to work faster so she could make a quick escape. Why had she said something to Cathy when she'd been home free? Deep down she knew why, but she didn't want to admit it. She needed a friend to help process this crazy mess. Someone who'd witnessed the entire story.

Cathy rounded the counter and faced Judy. "Don't think you're going to escape so easily."

"Judy," the barista called out.

Drats. It couldn't have been one minute sooner, could it?

"Cathy," the same girl called out only a few seconds later.

Cathy Mitchell clutched her cardboard coffee cup and handed

Judy hers. "Judy Gaylord, now you sit down and tell me what's going on. I can't believe I had to find out about this through idle gossip."

"I didn't know myself until last night." Judy cautiously sipped her hot tea then sat at the farthest table from the crowd.

Cathy plopped down across from her and tapped her fingers against the tabletop. "Well, I do declare, this is a crazy mess. You think James knew about you and his cousin and that's why he's been hiding down there in Miami?"

"Cathy, I don't need your attitude, I need my friend. The one that I lost all those years ago." Cathy opened her mouth to interrupt, but Judy quickly continued. "I know how you felt about James and that you think I took him away from you, but I didn't. We just...loved each other. You don't know how sorry I am that I hurt my best friend, but you never even went out with him. And you never told me how you felt about him until it was too late."

Cathy rolled her eyes. "Well, it's about time."

Judy dabbed at the droplet sliding down from the lid to the table. "What are you talking about? About time for what?"

"About time my best friend apologized for stealing my man." Cathy smiled then reached out and covered Judy's hands with hers. "Now, how are you handling all this?"

Judy's heart soared despite the churning in her stomach over James. Had her childhood best friend, the one she'd quarreled with for decades, really forgiven her? "You mean—"

"I mean our feud is on hiatus for a bit. That's all I'm saying." Cathy's familiar twang deepened for extra emphasis.

"Fine, a temporary truce. I'll take it." Judy smiled and squeezed her friend's hand, feeling a renewed connection.

"Now, are you going to face James today?"

Judy let out a long breath. "I already did."

Shock had Cathy's mouth dropping open. "Really? What did he say?"

Judy shook her head and took a sip of her tea before answering. "To get out."

Cathy gasped. "Is that all he said? And did you?"

Judy shrugged. "Eventually. I refused at first."

"At first? You mean you did leave? You?" Cathy shook her head. "I'm surprised the cops weren't called because you beat him over the head with a stupid stick."

Judy chuckled. "Well, I thought about it, but I couldn't. He wasn't James. Not the James I once knew. His eyes, they were..."

"What?"

Judy ran her finger around the edge of the lid. "Distant, lost... scared. I stayed partially to make sure he was okay, but also to demand he didn't leave Sweetwater County without speaking to me first."

Cathy leaned back in her chair. "You're as stubborn as ever, aren't you?"

Judy toyed with her napkin. "It's not that. He's got a life, one without me. Things happened, choices were made, and I can't change them now, but I want to know why. Perhaps it's not fair. Maybe I lost the right to know when I—"

"Hog wash." Cathy waved her hand with an air of royal command. "That's not the Judy I know. You march back there and face him. Tell him he wronged you for making you think he was dead all those years. I mean, who does that?"

Judy forced the lump in her throat down so she could speak. "We both know he didn't return here because he knew that I'd betrayed him. I should've remained true forever like I'd promised."

"You were kids. Five minutes is an eternity at that age. You've beat yourself up about this for the past forty years. Now, here's your chance to find forgiveness, if nothing else. You've thought all these years that I hated you for winning James' heart, but I didn't. You shut me out."

"What are you talking about?" Judy choked, trying not to make a public spectacle.

"I tried to comfort you after we received the news, but you wouldn't let me. You ran to Michael instead."

"You loved him, too. I didn't want to cry on your shoulder knowing I'd hurt you. Besides, I didn't run to Michael. I ran away from everyone. I didn't want to face the truth."

"And you've never stopped running." Cathy pressed her lips together.

Judy shook her head, worrying the napkin in front of her. "What do you mean?"

Cathy gripped her hand. "Stop murdering that napkin and I'll tell you."

Judy tossed the shredded paper aside and squared her shoulders, readying herself for a Cathy lecture. It was long overdue. "Go ahead."

"You've done a lot right in your life. That boy of yours is thoughtful, kind, tough, and turns the head of every girl in the county. You run a successful business. You're on about every board or committee in town and you would give the shirt off your back to help a stranger."

"But..."

"But you don't let anyone in. All these years I've tried to be your friend, but you're not easy to love, girl. Don't get me wrong. If someone else needs a shoulder to cry on, or money to pay a bill, you're there. But let someone know your inner thoughts, or try to connect with you, and you shut them out." Cathy sat back and crossed her arms over her chest, indicating the lecture was over.

Judy sat in the corner of the town coffee shop, facing an ugly truth about herself. Cathy Mitchell, the town gossip with nothing to do but poke her nose in everyone's business, really was a kind-hearted soul. Too bad she didn't want anyone knowing that.

"I'm sorry, Cathy. I didn't know."

"Well, now you do." Cathy stood and slid her purse strap over her shoulder. "If you need a friend, you know where to find me."

Cathy sauntered from the shop, leaving Judy with swirling thoughts of past lives and mistakes. Of friendships lost and what life she'd chosen to live. Cathy was right, she'd hidden behind the façade she'd created to shadow her shame all those years ago. To be that perfect woman despite the Scarlet Letter on her chest, but it was time to toss that letter away.

Chapter Four

A WARM GLOW AWAKENED JAMES, despite his longing to return to his dream world. One where he held the auburn-haired, lovely eyed beauty in his arms while they rocked in the swing on the front porch of his family home. It was the first night in as long as he could remember that only pleasant dreams danced in the morning fog of his mind, instead of the dark world that usually lurked in his subconscious.

He stretched the kinks from his back and neck then eyed the white wainscoting and light grey walls. In the morning light, the room looked almost homey and fresh, despite the few cobwebs.

How long had he slept? A few hours, perhaps. It didn't matter, he needed to find where his mother would've kept her old documents. She'd left everything behind when she'd moved to Miami, so if it was anywhere, it'd be in this house.

He stood, his calf aching from the previous evening's debacle. The image of Judy near him when he'd returned to reality caused his hands to shake once again. He took a deep breath and calmed his nerves. Rubbing the tension from his temples, he scanned his childhood room, forcing the thought of what could have happened from his mind.

The attic room hadn't changed much. Even his old football trophies still sat on top of the bookshelves he and his father had made when he was eleven. That was the year his parents let him move up to the top floor for more privacy.

Lifting a picture frame, he smeared the dust away to reveal an image of Judy, Cathy, himself, Michael, and two other friends at the local drive-in. They'd snuck some beer from Cathy's parents that night. Cathy had ended up in the woods, puking the entire time, while he and Judy made out in the back seat of his friend's old Corvette. Not that there was much room, but for two teens, it was enough.

He eyed the double bed he'd slept on last night. He and Judy had been up here once, when they were seventeen. He chuckled. *Mother nearly came undone.* He remembered Judy frantically re-buttoning her shirt, which had taken him an hour to convince her to let him unbutton. The talking-to they got that afternoon, not to mention the threat of telling Judy's father, an ex-military sharp shooter, kept them from any more undressing activities for a while.

Opening the window, he leaned out to look over the land. It was God's country. Beautiful rolling hills and over-grown pastures. The scent of fresh dogwood and magnolia blossoms filled the air. His heart warmed in a way it hadn't in decades. He'd stayed away for so long because he was afraid of what would happen. Exactly what happened last night. But somehow, today, in this light, anything seemed possible.

A squirrel skittered over the front porch roof, up the drain-pipe then onto the gable roof overhead. He leaned further out and looked up. The gutter was full of leaves and debris. It needed cleaning before the house ended up with water damage. The entire home needed work.

It didn't matter though. He'd be signing the property over to the county in a matter of hours, if he could find that document.

Gripping the window with his fingers, he yanked on it, but it didn't budge. He couldn't leave it open for the rodents to get in.

With a huff, he marched down to the main floor, avoiding the broken step, and went to the garage, hoping to find some WD-40. The door squeaked open into a world of wall-to-wall stacked old furniture and boxes.

Great. If the documentation was anywhere in the house, it'd probably be among this stuff. He slid one large box off the top and dropped it onto the country wood kitchen table. A spider crawled down the side, and he flicked it onto the floor.

He opened the top to discover it full of old photo albums. The faded covers with brocade decoration intrigued him, but he was on a mission, so he retrieved another box then another. Not one of them was marked indicating what was inside. This was going to take a lot longer than he'd anticipated.

"Hey, anyone back there?" A voice with a deep country drawl echoed from his past through the house, nudging a smile across his lips. He about faced on his heels. "Cathy?"

A rounded face with deep lines, but a bright, friendly smile, stood in the garage doorway. "Yeah, darling. It's me." It was an older, plumper version, but that twang and concerned brow was unmistakable. "So, I hear you've been hanging with the locals out here." She slid her thumb through a metal circle attaching a strap to her oversized purse and leaned against the wall. "What happened to your leg?"

The slight throb in his calf returned. "I fell. The step gave way." His head swarmed with thoughts of running. What the hell was he thinking coming back here?

"Calm down. You look like a deer on opening weekend of hunting season."

James shook his head and scooted around several boxes to the kitchen. Cathy took a step back to let him pass before she followed him into the front room. He leaned against the window molding and watched birds swoop down to capture their prey. His stomach growled so loud it sounded like a lion in the nearly empty room.

From behind, Cathy's shoes clicked closer. "After you change and clean up, we'll get you a bite to eat. You look like you need to get out of here."

James huffed. "It's not necessary. I'll make do. Besides, these are the only pants I brought. That son of Judy's is a persuasive young man. He swooped me up here before I even realized what was going on, or had time to pack."

"You expect anything less from a child of Judy?"

He chuckled. "No, I guess not. But still, I don't want to go into town. I just want to find the paperwork I need and get out of here." He shrugged. "Like I said, I'll make do.

"Make do with what? Cardboard? Now listen here, James Benjamin. Get over yourself, clean up and let's get you fed. After that, you can tell me why the hell you decided to come back here after swearing me to secrecy all these years."

Chapter Five

Judy dabbed cold water under her eyes then reapplied some mascara. Crying was becoming a habit, one she intended to stop immediately.

The front door of the antique shop jingled, alerting Judy to Lisa's arrival so she piled her cosmetics back into her bag, fluffed her bangs, pushed her shoulders back and painted on a smile. With one last deep breath, she marched out to the showroom. "Hi, there. How was your dinner with Eric last night?"

Lisa stood in the doorway with a big grin, Eric behind her.

"What are you two up to?" Judy ambled forward, stopping when Lisa raised her hand to show off a gorgeous diamond ring.

"Oh my God! It's beautiful." Judy clutched Lisa's hand, bringing it closer to her face to admire the ring. "When? How? Oh, I don't know what I'm saying. I'm so excited for you both." She flung herself into Eric's arms. "I'm so happy for you, son."

"Thanks, Mom. I'm happy for me, too." Eric chuckled.

Judy stepped back and playfully smacked his shoulder. "You didn't tell me."

Eric held his hands up in defense. "Sorry, I never had a chance.

I bought the ring while I was in Miami and I wasn't going to give Lisa a chance to change her mind."

Lisa turned her hand so she could see the ring better. "I'd only told him I was ready to consider getting married the night before he left."

"What a night that was." Eric tucked Lisa into his side. His gaze danced between the glowing woman at his side and his mother. "Lisa and I would like to take you to brunch. I've got one more present I'd like to give Lisa and I'd like you there for it."

Judy watched as Eric and Lisa stared into each other's eyes. Lord knows things hadn't worked out in the past for the Gaylords in the love department. It warmed her heart to see how happy and in love they were. "What are we waiting for? Lisa, flip the sign to *closed*. I'll grab my purse."

Eric cleared his throat, calling Judy's attention back to him. "You sure? I mean, I know you're facing a lot right now, with James in town and all."

Judy waved her hands dismissively and marched to the counter, grabbed her purse and stared them down. "You promised me brunch. Let's go. You know better than to stand up a lady."

Eric chuckled. "I'd never do that. My mother taught me better."

They filed out the front door and walked down to the café two blocks from the square. Entering the bustling restaurant, the hostess immediately seated them. Eric pulled out the chair for Lisa then Judy.

As they all sat quietly glancing over the brunch menu, Eric lifted Lisa's hand and kissed her fingers. Judy fought the tears that threatened, so much for no more crying. She might not have had her own happily-ever-after, but she'd be able to witness her only child's. Soon she'd even be a grandmother. Life was good, no reason to mess with perfection.

"You okay? You're quiet." Eric asked.

A waitress held up a pot of coffee. Lisa shook her head. "Decaf, please."

Judy lifted her cup for the waitress to pour. "Fully leaded, please." She quirked an eyebrow at Eric. "I'm fine. Why do you ask?"

"Because you're being quiet," Eric teased.

Judy lowered her cup to the table and watched the lady grab decaf for Lisa. "You stop, or I'll tell Lisa about the time you stripped naked and decided it would be funny to run through—"

"I take it back." Eric held up his hands in surrender.

Lisa giggled. "Oh, you can tell me at the store later. I've got to hear that one."

Eric huffed. "Great. I'm outnumbered. I need more men to back me up."

Judy watched as Eric's smile faded and Lisa fidgeted with the silverware in front of her. She shifted over in front of Lisa. "So, how'd he do it? Big balloons, roses, a choir singing under the moonlit sky?"

Eric shook his head and dropped his face in his hands. "Mom, you're killing me."

Lisa laughed aloud. "No, he took me to Franciscos."

"That amazing Italian place I've been begging him to take me to for the past five years?"

"Yep, that's the one." Lisa leaned into Eric. "I think we know where we're taking your mother for her birthday."

Eric sipped his coffee. "Oh, I'll make sure to do that or I'll never hear the end of it."

Judy shot him a playful sideways glance. "Well, you were *once* my favorite son."

"I'm your only son." Eric smiled and waved the waitress over. "But now that I've been firmly scolded like a young boy, I think we should eat."

The waitress greeted them. "What can I get for y'all?"

Judy set her menu down with a little extra enthusiasm. "We're celebrating here, so I'm going to splurge. I'll have the Eggs Benedict."

Lisa sighed. "I'll have fresh fruit and a bagel with cream cheese."

Eric gathered the menus and handed them to the waitress. "I'll have the Big Daddy Brunch. Oh, with the special side, please.

"Certainly, sir."

As the waitress skittered off behind the front counter, Judy said, "Okay, back to last night. So, how did he propose?"

Lisa slid her fingers through Eric's and he kissed her knuckles one by one. "He got down on one knee and asked me to marry him. It was romantic and sweet. He told me how he felt and I almost let him finish before I launched into his arms, knocking down the waiter."

Eric howled with laughter. "The poor guy spilled crab bisque all over another waiter."

Judy gasped. "I hope no one was hurt."

"No, not at all," Lisa said. "The staff clapped and helped us off the floor."

"Well, no points for originality, son," she winked at his shrug, "but you did good. Let's see that ring of yours again."

Lisa splayed her fingers on the table. "Oh, he did just fine." She beamed up at him.

Judy squeezed her son's hand resting on the tabletop. "Yes, you did good, son. Not just with the ring, but with your choice. I know you will both be happy together for many years to come."

Lisa shifted in her chair and gripped the table.

"You okay, hon?"

"Not to worry. Just a little back pain. No pre-term labor or anything."

A waiter approached with a small white pillow on top of a silver plate. "Perhaps this will help, ma'am." He lowered the plate to display a white satin pillow, trimmed with white lace with pink, swirling letters on it that read *Amelia Gaylord*.

Eric lifted the pillow from the plate and handed it to Lisa. "Last night I proposed to you. Today, I want you to know how much I'll love our little girl."

Tears pricked at Judy's eyes. Perhaps her son was more creative than she gave him credit for.

Chapter Six

JAMES WATCHED the trees go by on the endless road to town. Surprisingly, the drive soothed his soul, and the shaking in his hands finally stopped. "What have you been doing all these years?"

Cathy flipped on the turn signal and made her way toward the city limits. "Well, I didn't become no hot shot psychiatrist, but I've done fine. My husband left me well enough."

James eyed the faded welcome sign at the edge of town. *Welcome to Sweetwater County...where your home and heart belong.* He had believed that once. He cleared his throat and shifted in his seat, trying to stay focused on the truth, not the fantasy, of his youth. "Kids?"

"Yeah, but they aren't around here no more." Cathy's voice lowered, a sadness coating her words.

James brushed some of the dry sand from his right pant leg. "You see them much?"

She shook her head. "I'm afraid I'm just too much for my daughter-in-law. She hasn't invited me to their home since they moved. How 'bout you?"

"Never married."

"That don't mean you never had kids." Cathy winked.

"No, I guess it doesn't. I didn't, though."

Cathy tightened her grip on the steering wheel. "I'm not trying to drag up old memories, but can you tell me why you refused to see me? I mean, not right after, but I asked your mother several times."

James gripped his knee. "Too hard. The only way I could stay away was to sever all ties. I couldn't come back here. I just couldn't."

A few minutes of silence passed and James tried to keep his mind in the present. He'd made choices, and now he had to live with them.

Cathy slowed the car and turned into a parking lot. "I hope you like brunch food. This place has the best southern style breakfast in the entire county."

"Love it. Thanks." For the first time since arriving, a hunger rumbled in his stomach. He'd barely eaten anything, but last night was over and hunger was gripping his attention by the horns.

"Well, you could look a little happier, you know. I did save you from starving to death." She passed several open parking spaces until finding a spot in the back. "I hope you don't mind walking on that leg."

"It was just a splinter, I can manage."

When he opened the door, a chilly wind carried a fresh floral smell, reminding him of the flowers his mother and Judy planted outside the home the spring before he left.

Cathy came around the car and slipped her arm into his. "Come on. I'm hungry."

He wondered if he should remind her this wasn't a date, but it was best to avoid the subject. He'd rejected Cathy once. She'd reminded him of a cornered wild beast last time. Perhaps it was best to make it through the day and fly back in the morning.

He walked with a little distance between them. Despite her hand on his arm, she didn't move closer to him, which was a relief.

Drawing the door open, he found the café full of hustling wait staff and people eating.

Cathy drew him close to her side, but he slid from her embrace, stepped away and shoved his hands in his pants pocket. Rocking back and forth on his heels, he averted his gaze to the floor. "Listen. I don't want to give you the wrong idea. I-I don't—"

"Oh, relax, old man. I'm not puttin' the moves on ya."

The smell of frying bacon, eggs, and pancakes drew his attention. "Fine, but you sit on the other side of the table."

The hostess held up one hand. "Please, wait a moment here. We have something special going on and everyone's up out of their booths. Let them settle back down and then we'll seat ya."

"What's going on?" Cathy asked, peering around the girl.

The hostess stepped back so they could both see into the dining area. People backed away from a table, clearing the walk-way. James' eyes scanned between the individuals until it stopped on a man and woman in a loving embrace. It was Eric. A woman with auburn hair on the other side of the table, dabbed at her eyes with a white linen napkin...*Judy*.

"Congratulations! You're going to get a daughter and a grand-daughter all in one day." A thin, tall man shouted at Judy before he resumed his seat.

James shuffled past the hostess, his feet moving without his authority, his body drawn to the beauty in the booth. Breathing, walking, only the movement of his body registered.

Judy slapped her palm against the table. "Two weeks?" She shook her head. "How can we plan a wedding in two weeks?"

"We can have it in the shop, or in the middle of the street, I don't care," Lisa blubbered.

Eric glanced up then slid from the booth, offering his hands. "Hey, old man. How's it going? Join our celebration."

Judy turned and slid from the booth, too. He wasn't sure if it was because of the distraction of his episode, or the dim lighting, but today, in the daylight, she was even more breathtaking than he remembered.

The world around them slowed to a stop. Her lips slightly apart, her blue eyes with strands of silver disappeared behind large dark pupils, her hair the color of the most beautiful sunset.

"James?" Judy's lips trembled. She teetered and he caught her arm before she stumbled.

Her skin was as soft as he remembered. Heat shot from his hand up his arm and through his body.

"Judy." he rasped.

Chapter Seven

JUDY HELD tight to his hand. If she let it go, he might disappear forever again.

Eric moved beside them. "You okay?" he asked.

Judy couldn't form words, thoughts, movement. She just held *his* hand.

She locked gazes with the man in front of her. A man more handsome than she'd remembered. In the dim light last night, she hadn't truly appreciated him. The lines on his face distinguished his brow and the silver flattop made his eyes shine. If it was possible, the man in front of her was more breathtaking than the eighteen year old she once loved. Yet, behind his silver eyes was a darkness. The innocence of youth had faded.

"Wow." James' hand lifted to her cheek, but dropped back to his side before making contact.

She somehow managed to stand on her own, yet didn't release his warm, strong hand. Tearing her gaze away, she took him in from his silver hair to his torn pant leg, covered in dry blood. His broad shoulders had filled out, but his waist had remained thin.

Questions flooded her mind but would he answer them now? *Where have you been? Why did you leave? Do you hate me? Can you ever forgive me?* But none of them reached her mouth. She cleared her throat. "Your leg okay?"

Everyone looked at her. After over forty years, all she could manage was to ask him about his leg, but at that moment, it was the only question she had the courage to face the answer to, and she worried if she pushed, he'd only flee.

"Yes, I think the step is worse off than I am." His fingers squeezed her hand, the same way they once did when they were young.

"Does it hurt?"

He shrugged. "Stings a little."

A server squeezed between them and the table. The sound of dishes clanking and people chattering slowly invaded, bringing her back to reality.

"Cathy brought me here to eat. I'm taking a break from finding proof of life." He shook his head and chuckled. "Still seems so silly."

"What part?" Judy longed to know more, but the way his eyes scanned the room and his hands trembled, she didn't dare push.

He stepped back, taking his hand with him. "I should go." Then pushing his shoulders back, he turned to Eric. "Congratulations, kid," he said before swaggering away.

Cathy stood watching them from the doorway. She'd brought him here? Why? Before she could think to ask, Cathy retreated after James, sitting together in a booth at the back of the café.

His warmth...those silver eyes that once mesmerized her, the swagger of his hips and the strength of a giant...all gone. In one second, a connection of warmth through her body and soul had returned, and in the next, all of it disappeared, just like before.

Eric's hand slipped to her elbow. "Come on. I'll take you home."

Numbness filled her. *Go after him. Talk to him*, her mind urged. She fought for control of her body, to move her feet, to open her mouth and call out to him, but nothing happened. Instead, she focused on the soft, white pillow on the table, abandoned while her son and soon-to-be daughter-in-law came to her rescue.

"Judy," Lisa said.

A quick scan of the café told her that James' and her reunion stirred more attention than Eric's special gift. She shook off the fog and slid her elbow from Eric's hand. This was their time, not hers, and she refused to ruin it. "Don't be silly. Sit. We have some celebrating to do."

Lisa reached to embrace her, but Judy retreated to her side of booth, her body rejecting any touch. No hand or hug would suffice now that she'd felt James again. Slowly, her lungs opened and allowed a full breath. "Please, sit."

Lisa's eyes lowered and Eric held her hand while she gently lowered back into her seat, all the time keeping his gaze fixed on Judy. Lifting the glass of orange juice the waitress must have delivered while her attention was elsewhere, she held it high. "To you two and my soon-to-be granddaughter. Life is such a gift." Her voice cracked, and she took a sip of juice. She focused on the fresh pulp sliding down her throat while the waitress plopped her plate of Eggs Benedict in front of her. "Wow, two weeks? Really? Have you thought of where you want to have the ceremony?"

Eric finally lifted his glass, taking a long draw. With a swipe of his tongue across his lips, he placed his glass on the table. "We haven't gotten that far yet. Right, Hon?"

Lisa shrugged. "Courthouse?"

"What? Not for my soon-to-be daughter. What about the Barn?"

Lisa's eyes sparkled. "The community center? It's where we had our first dance. Do you think it'll be available?"

"I'll make sure it is." Judy winked. "You two are a big deal in this town. I think we could all use something to celebrate." Sadness crept into her voice and she cleared her throat.

Lisa wrapped her fingers around Judy's but she nudged them away. "Don't. Not now." She picked up her fork and toyed with the white egg, swirling it through the hollandaise sauce on her plate. "Not here, not now. Let me concentrate on you two."

Eric stabbed some scrambled egg. "So, don't you ladies need to figure out the flowers or something?"

Lisa ran her fingers across the lace of the pillow. "And a dress. How am I going to find a non-white dress big enough to fit a house?"

Eric's brow furrowed. "Why not white?"

Lisa pointed at her belly. "Uh, hello?"

Judy waved dismissively. "You'll wear whatever color you want. And as for being a house, you're not big at all, dear. Your arms and legs are still perfect. I say you wear white, something that shows off that beautiful belly of yours. People are gonna talk. Might as well make it about how beautiful you are."

Lisa blushed and Eric laughed aloud. "Mom's always right. Remember that."

Lisa smiled. "Okay, white and an empire waist it is."

Eric held her forearm, brushing his thumb back and forth over her skin. "It doesn't matter if you wear a potato sack. You'd still be the most beautiful girl on the planet."

Judy picked up her fork and scooted some food around her plate. "I'll go tomorrow morning and see about the barn and then we can look for a dress. Actually, Cathy is an excellent seamstress. Perhaps she can make your dress."

Lisa shot a sideways glance at her. Eric stopped his fork half way to his mouth, the pierced potato dangling in midair.

Judy avoided eye contact and kept her attention on her meal. When they finished their food, Eric walked them back to the store. A lively spring wind made the *J &L Antiques* sign squeak. It was a peaceful day out, with no storm clouds in the sky.

Judy scooted by Eric and Lisa as they kissed and opened the door. Flipping the sign over, she did her best to focus on business.

For the rest of the day, customers came in and left, but Judy couldn't recall who they were or what they had purchased.

Lisa returned from the back kitchen. "I love you, too. I'll see you tonight." She lowered the phone from her ear.

Judy shook the fog that had haunted her all afternoon away, noticing Lisa's brows furrow as she rubbed her head. "You should sit."

"We should both sit." Lisa pulled out a chair and lowered with a little extra care. "You've looked like you were about to face a firing squad all afternoon. As if you're stuck in some sort of long loop in your head, reliving what brought you to this moment. Don't get me wrong. I completely understand. I'm just here if you want to talk. We can go ahead and close up. It looks like most people are done shopping for the day."

Judy scooted a chair next to Lisa and joined her. "I'm fine."

Lisa's eyebrow rose. "Really? Then why did you double charge one client, break a vase, and worst of all, forget your afternoon tea?"

Judy chuckled. "That's why I'm in such a daze. See, problem solved."

"Judy Gaylord. Now, you listen to me. I've had to spill my guts to you from day one. Now, it's your turn."

"I've told you more than anyone else," Judy huffed.

Lisa took a long breath. "I know it's hard for you to talk about, so I've never pushed. Yet, things have changed. Why haven't you made James answer your questions? That's not like you."

Judy leaned back in her chair. "There're several reasons. Part of me wants to know he had a good life, that I didn't ruin it for him. Another part of me is angry. I want answers, but every time I look into his eyes, I don't know if I can face the truth. There's so much pain in him."

"What do you want to know?"

Judy shot up and paced around the table. "Why he didn't tell me he was alive? Why didn't he come back? Did he think I would've turned him away?"

Lisa caught her arm. "Would you have? You're an honorable woman. Do you think you would've left Eric's father if James had returned?"

Judy sighed. "I...I don't know."

"If you have questions, so will James." Lisa squeezed her arm. "You should prepare yourself for what you want to say, as well as what you want to know. That fear in his eyes may have nothing to do with you. From what Eric said, James suffered a lot during the war and he's been running from demons ever since."

"I hadn't thought of that." Judy fell back onto her chair. Seeing Lisa worry her bottom lip, she said, "You don't need this stress. Now, let's forget about this nonsense and call it an early day." Judy rose and crossed the store to the front door. She couldn't help but hesitate and search the walkways for James before she flipped the sign to *closed*.

Lisa's footsteps approached from behind. "If there was a chance for you to know more before you confronted James, would you want that opportunity?"

Judy retrieved her sweater from the antique wooden coat rack. "What are you talking about? His father died years ago and shortly after, his mother turned the house over to Walter to manage, saying she was retiring to a warmer climate."

"Eric told me that James said something peculiar when he found him in Florida. We discussed it, but we're both unsure if we should tell you. It could hurt you deeply and neither of us want that. But at the same time, we think it could help."

Judy slipped her hands into the sleeves of her sweater and faced the younger woman. "I want to know."

Lisa took an exaggerated breath. "His being alive wasn't a total secret. Someone else in town knew."

Judy clutched the doorknob. "Well, I guess that doesn't surprise me. His mother had plenty of friends in town." She turned back to Lisa. "I want to know who it was. If this person or people are still alive I'd like to talk to them. I think it would help if I understood a few things before I saw James again. Do you know who it was?"

"Cathy Mitchell. She's known this entire time that James was alive. But I don't know what happened, or why she kept the secret from you."

Judy held onto the knob for dear life as the room spun, her head feeling as though it might float away. "What do you mean *she knew?*"

Lisa placed a hand on her back. "Please. Let's talk about this. I'm here for you."

Judy swallowed the rise of anger and hatred boiling up from her stomach. "Thank you, but if it's talking, that I'll be doing with Cathy."

Yanking the door open, she marched down Main Street. Her hands shook and her jaw popped under the pressure. In all her life, she couldn't recall ever being angry enough to cause physical harm to another human being, until now.

§

JAMES SAT DOWN AT THE KITCHEN TABLE, PREPARING TO SEARCH the hundredth box when his phone rang from the front foyer. He trotted through the house and snatched his phone from the top of some stacked boxes.

"Hello?"

"Hey, Old Man. How's the search going?" Eric's voice filled his ear.

"Well, kid—" James rubbed the back of his neck. "I think I might have found where my mother kept her stuff."

"That's good news."

James meandered back to the kitchen. "You'd think, but not if you saw the mountain of boxes I needed to go through."

"I see. Well, if you want a hand, I'm headed your way

tomorrow to drop off some contracts. I'll stop in and lend some muscle."

James eyed the mound of work. "You saying I can't lift a box?"

"You are an old man, but if you don't—"

"Hold your horses. You drug me all the way here. I'm thinking you owe me. Bring food and I'll let you help."

"You got it."

James hit *end* and slid the phone into his pocket.

What are you doing? The boy might be a great kid, but he's still Judy's son.

Stepping back into the garage, he maneuvered between an old, busted chair and a dresser. He'd forgotten they'd added an extension onto the garage. His dad loved restoring old cars, and according to his mother, he'd buried himself in the hobby after finding out his son was dead.

James drew in a long breath of musty air and leaned against the corner of his father's antique desk covered in dust and grime. Yep, this was too big a task for one person. He just needed Eric's help, that was all. James would avoid all conversation of Judy and concentrate on finding the document and getting himself out of Sweetwater County.

Chapter Eight

THE DOOR JINGLED, alerting Judy to Lisa's presence.

"Wow, you rearranged the store, and cleaned it. Were you here all night?" Lisa stored her purse behind the counter and eyed Judy suspiciously.

"I came in a couple hours ago. I didn't move that much." Judy retrieved her purse and slung the strap over her shoulder. "Can you handle the store for a bit? I won't be gone more than an hour or so. I'm headed to the Parks and Recreation department to fill out a formal facility request for the Barn and then I have a stop to make."

Lisa tried to put her hands on her hips, but they only slid off. "A stop? You mean you're going to confront Cathy."

Judy tightened her grip on the leather strap of her purse. "Yes. I. am."

"Should I send Sheriff Mason to her house?"

Judy fidgeted with the ceramic cat on the edge of the wood desk. "No need. The coward wouldn't meet me at home when I tried to corner her yesterday. Said there wouldn't be any witnesses."

"What did you say to that?"

"That if I really wanted to kill her she'd be dead and they'd never find the body." Judy didn't give Lisa a chance to respond before she marched out the front door then down the street to the Parks and Recreation office. Shielding her eyes from the morning sun, she dodged the early morning foot traffic and turned down Baker to the back alley and over two more streets.

Entering the county offices building, she spotted Stella, the knitting store owner, sitting on a long bench filling out some paperwork.

"Hi, Judy." Stella waved, but her brows were furrowed in concern. Yep, the entire town knew by now about her epic fail, lost love, and pending murder of her ex-best friend.

Judy put on her most convincing fake smile and waved. "Hey, Stella. Beautiful day."

"Where're you off to in such a hurry?"

"You mean you haven't heard? My Eric and Lisa are getting married." Judy still didn't stop. If she did, she'd be caught in the endless questions of the gossip web. "Sorry, I have to run. I need to fill out a facility request. I hope we'll see you at the Barn two weeks from today."

"I'll be there. Tootles."

Two turns to the right and she plowed into the rec department, snagged a form from the metal file box hanging from the wall, filled it out and slapped it on Ruth's desk. "Can you process this for me, please?"

"Um, sure." Ruth glanced down at the form. "It'll cost ya two hundred dollars. Whatcha need the Barn for? It's mostly reserved for city events, corporate functions, and weddings."

Judy unzipped her purse and made a check out to *Creekside Parks and Recreation*. "That's right. And yes, I want to rent it."

"Oh...my...god! You're getting married? I mean, I heard of course, but after all these years?"

Judy's mouth went dryer than a field after the fall harvest.

"You finally get your happily-ever-after. Not many of us—"

Judy shot a hand up. "Form. Process. Please. It's not my wedding. Eric and Lisa are getting married."

Ruth's already rosy cheeks turned a deep crimson. "Oh...well, I dare say, I'm so sorry. I just thought...oh, um...Let me check the calendar. Just a sec."

Some of Judy's anger deflated, replaced by a strange emptiness in her belly.

Ruth stamped the form, tore off the bottom copy and handed it to Judy. "You're lucky. Nothing's going on that night. Um...about what I said. I'm sorry—"

Judy folded the form and backed away from the counter. "No apology necessary. I'm just thankful the Barn was available. We hope you can join us for the wedding. Lisa wants to invite the entire town. Of course, I have a ton to do if I'm going to help her pull this off. Please excuse me."

"Yes, of course. Let me know if I can help," Ruth shouted after Judy as she flew out the door.

This town's gone nuts. What made them all think James returned for her? At this point, it seemed more likely he'd returned to see Cathy. The one that knew he was alive all these years.

Judy stormed down Main, nearly knocking over Mr. Peterson. She wasn't going to wait for lunch, it was time to face Cathy Mitchell, the traitor, and she knew exactly where to find her. To think, she'd almost attended the Fourth of July planning committee meeting under the guise of friendship. She would've been there right now, sitting by Cathy, picking out what band would play, what events would be held, if she hadn't discovered the truth.

Eyeing the coffee shop, she was thankful she could walk there. If she'd driven, she might have been tempted to run her ex-friend over. Yanking the door open, she spotted Cathy in line, waiting to order her coffee. Heat surged over her skin, her breath came short and quick and her hands shook. As if she was a pinball, just launched into action, she marched by two committee members, knocking one into the other, nudged past a table then a chair and a person in line before reaching the end of her journey.

Standing behind Cathy, she tapped her on the shoulder. When Cathy's smug face turned around, Judy lost it. Her hand was possessed. It cocked back and thrust forward, making contact with Cathy's face. Not even her comfy nursing-style shoes kept her upright.

She hit Cathy so hard the heavy woman stumbled, her body slamming into a table, sending beverages everywhere. Her feet flew over her head and she landed on her back on the ground.

Cathy moaned and cupped her cheek. "What the—"

"You lied to me. All these years of running your mouth all over town, and you chose the most important secret of my life to keep?" Judy shouted, with no regard to the shop full of witnesses. Wanting blood, she lunged forward, but someone grabbed her from behind.

Firm yet gentle hands grasped her biceps. "Mrs. Gaylord, please." Marcus' accented voice pleaded.

Cathy scrambled to her feet with the assistance of two women from out of town. "You've lost your mind. What the hell are you talking about?"

"You know very well what I'm talking about. James. You knew all these years he was alive!" Judy's entire body shook with rage. She yanked her arms, but Marcus wouldn't give. "You kept him from me. I deserved to know the truth."

Cathy shoved off the two women and stood straight, puffing out her chest. "You. You! It's always about you. What about him? He returned fragile beyond belief. The strong man that left us for war came home broken. He wouldn't have been good enough for the perfect princess that always had her way."

"Jealousy? That's what this is about? You kept him from me because you wanted him for yourself? Newsflash, you didn't get him either."

"You know nothing," Cathy sneered. "I didn't keep his secret

SPRING IN SWEETWATER COUNTY

for me. I kept it for him. For his family. It wasn't about you. By the time he returned, you were pregnant and married to his cousin."

"You should have told me."

"Why? So you could break Michael's heart, too? You two might have married out of obligation, but Michael loved you. I wasn't going to let you rip apart your family to run after a man that you couldn't have anymore."

"I would've helped him."

"You couldn't have. No one could. Not then. You have no idea what he went through. He spent six months in a bamboo cage after being captured by the Vietcong. He was tortured, starving, and watching all his comrades die. His mother had him committed when he almost killed her while they slept. She gave up everything to protect you, your child, and your husband. Even after all you did to that family, she still loved you. They all did. Every sacrifice made was for you and James. You weren't there. You have no idea how much that family suffered because of the war, and because you ran into the arms of another man a second after the one you professed to love was reported dead."

Judy recoiled, the fight draining from her body. She glanced around at all the people who'd gathered to watch the show. Neighbors and friends communicated in hushed whispers about her epic failure in life, her ultimate betrayal.

Marcus released her and she clutched the chair in front of her to stay upright.

Taking several deep breaths, Cathy stepped forward. "Judy."

She only raised a hand to stay Cathy's advance. "You made me apologize when all this time you lied to me. You're not a friend." Shaking her head, she shuffled out the door, down the walkway to her car.

As much as it still hurt that her ex-friend had lied to her, she knew Cathy spoke the truth. She'd done this. It was nobody's fault but her own.

Chapter Nine

JAMES SAT at the kitchen table with his head in his hands. It was early, and his head already throbbed.

For a second, the chirping and squawking of renewed spring life made him believe anything was possible, but what did he want? *It's best that I get out of Sweetwater County as soon as possible before I hurt someone again.* He pushed from the table to search more boxes, but his muscles protested so he fell back into his chair. His eyes felt heavy. A good night sleep would calm his nerves, but would tonight bring images of the auburn beauty or night terrors of the past?

"Hey, you."

James spun around to find Cathy in the doorway. "What? How'd...?"

Cathy took a seat by his side. "You were in that world of yours again and didn't even hear me arrive. Has it always been this way?"

James scrubbed his face. "No. When I'm at work down in Miami, I'm focused. I help the men returning from war. I'm a great doctor."

Cathy smiled. "I'm sure you're an amazing psychiatrist. Too bad you won't let anyone help you."

James shrugged. "I'm fine. I just need to get out of here before anything bad happens."

"Oh darling, it's a little late for that." Her hand rubbed the side of her face over a spot that looked like it had too much rouge. "That girl of yours packs quite a punch...literally."

He gasped. "She hit you?"

"Knocked me over a table." Cathy huffed. "Would've done worse than that if Marcus hadn't pulled her off."

James dug his thumbnail into the tabletop, flicking a stray piece of flaking stain. "She's mad, huh?"

Cathy waved her hands with a dramatic flair. "Mad? She's madder than a mule chewing on bumblebees."

"I warned the kid not to tell her. Don't worry, I won't stay. I'll be leaving in the morning, as soon as I can."

"First, you're gonna answer a few of my questions." She leaned closer. "Do you still love Judy? Why didn't you ever marry? Why didn't you let me visit you? And the most important question, why the hell did you decided to come back here after swearing me to secrecy all these years?"

ꙮ

JUDY TOOK A DEEP BREATH, INHALING THE FLORAL SCENT OF freshly planted flowers in the window box of the Southern Style Café. The warmth of the early afternoon sun heated her back, nudging her toward the door.

Now that she'd had time to cool off, she'd promised herself, and Cathy, this meeting would be more civil. If she didn't reign in her temper, she'd never find out about what happened to James and why he decided to keep his return a secret. With one last cleansing breath, she opened the door to the bustling café. Cathy already sat at a booth, gripping her coffee mug for dear life.

"Well, at least you showed. I'll admit I had my doubts." Judy slid into the bench across from her.

Cathy held up one palm. "Just remember, we're gonna behave like ladies, not fighting hens."

"Then I'll warn you, I didn't sleep a wink last night, but I'll do my best."

Cathy nodded. "It's time we cleared the air."

"You think? After all this time?" Judy let the sarcasm drip from her words before softening her tone. "Are you going to tell me the truth this time, or are you just going to lie?"

Cathy's head shot up, her mouth falling open. "I never lied to you."

"Grammar, that's all that is. You kept the fact that the love of my life was alive and living in Miami. Why? Why did you do that?"

"It wasn't my choice to make."

A white apron floated at the edge of the table, interrupting her drive to punch Cathy for a second time.

"Can I get you something?" the waitress asked.

Cathy smiled. "Good morning, Ansley. I'll take a sweet tea, please."

"Me too, please," Judy mumbled, keeping her eyes on Cathy.

"Certainly."

As the young woman in the pink and white uniform disappeared behind the counter, Judy said, "You were my friend, you should have told me. I had a right to know."

Cathy shook her head, her voice small. "Did you? I mean, you were pregnant with another man's baby. His cousin's."

Judy unfolded the napkin and smoothed the wrinkles out on her lap. "You told me you never judged me."

"I didn't. I never have. What happened was awful, terrible. You were grieving and so was Michael. It was something that just happened. But after all James went through, I couldn't expose him to more heartache and loss. You didn't see him."

"No, I didn't, because I didn't know he lived. You spent time with him after the war while I mourned his death."

A glass of amber liquid slid in front of Judy. "I'll have a Greek salad, please." Not that she wanted any food, but the quicker she ordered, the quicker the woman would go away.

"You?" Ansley looked to Cathy.

"I'll have the hamburger with a side salad."

"I'll have that right up for you."

The waitress moved on, but before Judy could continue, Cathy held up a palm. "Can you let me speak for a minute please? I promise if you still want to kill me, I'll hand you this steak knife when I'm done." Cathy waved the blade then set it to the far side, away from Judy.

Smart woman. "And drive us out to the middle of the valley?"

Cathy nodded. "I'll even dig my own grave. Now, listen up. I didn't spend time with James after the war. No one did. Not even his mother and father. You see, he tried to come home. To win you back, but he couldn't. The night he came back to Sweetwater, I was at the farmhouse. You'd been so down, and I was worried about you and the baby, so I went there to plan a surprise baby shower for you. Martha also wanted to be involved, to show you how much she loved and supported you."

At the thought of Martha not hating her, planning a shower for the baby instead, warmed Judy's heart for a second, but the look in Cathy's eyes warned that was the only good part of the story.

"That night, when I was there, James showed. No one knew he was coming. His parents hadn't even been notified about him being alive. It was joyous for about an hour, until everything went to hell in a handbasket." She pinched the bridge of her nose. "James wasn't the man who left to go to war. In his place, an animal returned. He behaved like a cornered, snarling beast. Nearly killed his mama."

Judy gasped. "What?"

Cathy lowered her hand. "I shouldn't be telling you this. It's his story to share, or not."

"Cathy Marie Mitchell. Spill it, or I swear—"

Cathy held up both hands in defense. "He held her by the throat. Pinned her against a wall and shouted crazy talk. He thought he was still at war, and she was part of a Vietcong group that had murdered his friends. His pa had to physically restrain him. If it wasn't for the fact James was undernourished and weak, he would've killed her."

"You were there during this?"

Cathy nodded. "It was like nothing I'd ever seen, or ever want to see again."

Judy wrung her hands. "What happened? Did they call the police?"

Cathy kept her gaze downcast. "No, I wish. His mama wouldn't hear of it. She was gonna save her son. After all, he'd made it home from the war in one piece. Her determination lasted far beyond anyone else's. His pa started calling people, specialists, careful not to let anyone in town know he was back. He feared James would murder you and Michael in your sleep. They hid all the knives, guns, and anything sharp, sleeping with their bedroom door locked. When James wasn't having an episode, he only sat in a dark room rocking in his old grandfather's chair. His mama tried to snap him out of it, and thought she was making progress until the night..."

Judy reached to take Cathy's hands, willing her to continue, but instead sat back and crossed her arms. Her feet tapped vigorously against the floor. "What night?"

Cathy looked up, locking gazes with her. "He busted down their bedroom door and throttled his mother. His pa finally had to pick up a baseball bat to get him off her. The next morning, he was gone."

"To where?"

Cathy inhaled deeply. "To a mental hospital out west. They specialized in post-war trauma. They tried to get him into the veteran's hospital, but the government claimed that Post Traumatic Stress Disorder didn't exist. Eventually, PTSD became a real diagnosis with the VA. Heck, part of that was due to James."

Judy's stomach rolled. He'd been here in Sweetwater County, alive. "I had a right to know."

"No, Judy, you didn't. It wasn't about you. What do you think would've happened if James found out about you and his cousin when he first got home? In the beginning, the only reason he agreed to go for treatment was to be better for you. His mama lived in fear that you'd show up at the house with the baby before he left."

Judy stared at her for a moment. "That's why she disowned me."

Cathy sat forward. "Yes. I urged her to tell you the truth later, but she said you'd found a little piece of happiness and she didn't want to take that from you."

"I would've—"

"Would have what? Left Michael? Broken up your family? I don't think so. Not in that day. And even if you did, James didn't deserve to be put through anything more than he had been."

Judy slammed her fists down on the table, ignoring the heads flipping in her direction. "You wanted him for yourself. That's why you kept the secret. You were always jealous of us." Cathy only smiled, which drove Judy's anger more. "You don't deny it?"

"No, I don't. But that isn't the reason I kept his secret."

"So, you just secretly visited him all these years? What about Randy? Did he know? Did you sneak off for secret rendezvous?"

"Judy Ann Gaylord. I know you're angry, but don't you dare accuse me of such things. I never saw James again, and you know I was faithful to my Randy. I didn't see James again until he arrived here in Sweetwater two days ago."

Judy unfurled her fists. "What are you saying?"

"He wouldn't see anyone, not even his mother. Not for years. It wasn't until he moved to Miami after finishing his Ph.D. in Psychiatry that he even saw his parents again. He kept in contact via mail and phone, but never in person. James didn't trust himself. He wouldn't dare risk anyone's life again. He's lived alone all these years. Afraid of what he might do in the middle of the night."

"Hey, you two. Looking a little intense over here." Eric stood next to their table looking down at them. They'd been so caught up in their conversation that she hadn't seen him enter the café. "Um... I take it you two were a bit loud. You've got an audience."

Judy glanced around the room and took a long steadying breath. "I guess that was me."

"You think?" Cathy chuckled. "You care to join us? It might save my life."

Eric smiled. "I'd love to join you ladies, but I'm supposed to take some food to James and help him find some documentation."

Judy's gut clenched tight. "You're going to the farm?"

Eric nodded. "He needs to find documentation to prove he's alive so he can deal with ownership of the farm."

Judy worried the hem of her shirt. "You looking through the house to find it?"

"Yes. Apparently, there are tons of boxes and he needs some help. I figured I'd lend him a hand. I hope that's okay with you."

"Of course." Judy forced a smile. "Um...there's a secret compartment in his mother's closet. Far back right corner. You'll need to push the door for it to spring open. If Martha had something important to keep, it'd be there."

Eric's phone buzzed. "Great. I'll just go grab the food I ordered and be on my way. Have a good one. And Mom, please don't make me bail you out of jail later. I'm a great attorney, but murdering Cathy in public is too much for even me to get you sprung from."

He slid his thumb up his phone, looking at the display as he sauntered to the cash register.

"I'm not happy with you," Judy said quietly, "and I'm not sure we'll ever be friends like we once were, but you're right. It wasn't your secret to tell. I just don't understand why later he didn't find me. I mean, once he was better."

Cathy pressed her lips together in a thin line.

"What is it?"

"James never got better. He just learned to ignore it all. Martha believed he never faced real life. He's hidden behind that degree and helping others, but never really rejoined society."

Judy's chest ached with sadness.

Eric set the bag of food on the table. "Hey, I have a huge favor to ask. Cathy, would you mind delivering this food to James. Oh, and tell him about the secret compartment. I've been called back to my office."

"Certainly."

Before Cathy could reach for the bag, Judy stood. "Don't be so transparent, son." She snagged the bag. "You don't have to beat a dead horse. I know you want me to speak with him. Well, here it goes."

Chapter Ten

An hour and five boxes later, the sound of gravel crunching under a car tire, followed by a rap at the front door drew James' attention from the mountain of boxes.

"Come in," he hollered.

The front door squealed open.

"In the kitchen. You better have brought some food, kid. I'm starved."

"I did bring food, but I'm afraid I'm not...kid."

A soft voice caressed his ears. Great, he knew this house would cause him to take a trip to crazy town. His pulse thudded against his neck. *Deep breath...in and out.*

"I think it's a burger and fries. You know, small town grease and all."

Judy...her voice...like a bird's song on the first day of spring. His chest tightened. One last deep breath, and with his eyes pressed tight, he swiveled to face the doorway. Peeking through his dark lashes, he found burgundy heels supporting strong legs and curved hips. He didn't need to search any further. "Judy?"

The heels shuffled closer. "Yes. I hope it's okay. Eric was called away. I'm here to help."

Here to help? The way she held her body stiff, her hands clutching the white grease stained bag tight, her speech slow and direct with a deep sorrow. Those were loaded words. "You're not talking about boxes, are you?"

"I know you must hate me. I once hated myself. If you'd just let me—"

"No explanation needed. Feel free to leave the food and head back to town. You shouldn't be here."

"If you didn't want me here, you wouldn't have come to Sweetwater."

James fisted his hands. "Your son tricked me."

"If he's so awful, why'd you invite him here, tell him to bring food and help you search the boxes? No, you would've kept him at arm's length. If you hate me, yell at me. Tell me I'm a cheap whore."

His gut wrenched at her words. "Don't."

"Don't what?" She stepped closer.

The room closed in around him, as if the universe demanded they be together. It had always been that way, and always would be. "You're not—"

Judy dropped the bag on the kitchen table between two boxes. "I made a promise to you and at the first test of my love, I betrayed you."

"Promises are just words meant to deceive someone, and mean little in this world. That's something I've known for a long time." That dark shadow moved over his soul, the one that nearly suffocated him with sadness and guilt. His throat tightened.

A gentle hand brushed his forearm and the shadow drifted off a smidgen, allowing a hint of light in. He wanted to pull her into his arms and hold her close, to force the shadow away forever, but it wasn't possible. He cleared his throat and scooted his chair back. "I've done things. You...you can't be near me. I won't chance it...ever."

"Your mother, I know."

He stiffened. "I see small town gossip already made its rounds. How my secret ever remained hidden from Sweetwater County until now, I'll never know."

Her hand moved from his arm and hung in midair for a moment. She entered his space, her full lips pressed together, her chest rose and fell. With one fluid movement, her hand slid around his waist and she embraced him. "I'm not scared of you. You won't hurt me."

For a moment, life seemed possible. One in a home instead of a half-unpacked apartment, with kids, grandkids, working the land, and friends coming in and out of the house all day. He swallowed the lump down, but couldn't bring his arms around her. He hadn't touched a woman for more than a one-night stand, always leaving before darkness came. Judy wasn't a one-night stand. She was everything, and he couldn't live with himself if he broke her.

"It's okay. You're home now."

He flew away from her, knocking over his chair, panting. "No, I can't stay."

Hurt flashed across her face. He wanted to pull her back against him and beg her forgiveness for all the lost years, but he couldn't.

Judy straightened. "I see. Well, let's eat and find your documentation so you can head back to Miami. I'm sure you have a great life there."

Great life? He had the one he'd planned, but great?

Judy slipped the burger wrapped in brown parchment out of the bag and set it on the table as he retrieved the chair, cursing himself for being so abrasive. "I-I'm sorry. I just..."

Judy smiled, one of her famous reassuring but I'm-not-letting-you-off-the-hook smiles. "Well, if you're not staying, and you claim not to hate me, at least sit and tell me why you never returned, or told me you were alive."

Most women would run yelling from the house over his little

fit. Not Judy. She'd always been a spit-fire, fearless and a pillar of strength to boot.

"Sit and start talking. When you're done, I'll tell you where the documents are."

"You know?"

Judy took a fry and nibbled it like it was the best thing she'd ever tasted. Not so much had changed over the years after all. "Yep, I think I know."

"Then tell me."

Judy cocked her hip and set her hand on it. "Now, it might have been awhile, but you should know how stubborn I am, so spill it."

James struggled with the words. How did he tell her what a monster he was? His fingers began to tremble as the memories flooded in.

"Here, sit." Judy took his hand and guided him to the chair. "Take it slow. Only tell me what you can manage."

"What if I can't manage any of it?" he breathed. Normally, at this point, his heart would be pounding so hard and his muscles so tight he'd feel like he was having a heart attack, but somehow he managed to stay relatively calm.

"Look at me. Keep your focus here, your eyes on me."

"That's a technique for dealing with PTSD."

She winked. "I know. I'm smarter than you think."

He settled in his chair and eyed the burger. The slop didn't look too appetizing after all. "Okay." He steadied his hands on his knees and gazed at Judy. "One night, toward the end of the war, I needed a break from my foxhole. The heat, bugs, rodents, smell, all of it. There had been reports of Vietcong in the area. They were like something out of a paranormal movie, able to move from place to place undetected. Stealth doesn't even begin to describe it." His eyes flicked nervously downward. "There were stories about men who blinked and the man next to him would be scalped without a sound. I knew better than to leave my men, but I left anyway and went for a walk. When I returned..." His heart thrashed against his sternum and he fought to remain in the present.

"Look at me, James. I'm right here with you. I'm not going anywhere." Her hand stroked his forearm, soothing his tension.

He cleared his throat. "All my friends, my comrades were slaughtered. I was captured, imprisoned in a bamboo cage at a Vietcong camp. Six months later, the Vietcong abandoned their camp during a conflict. A Vietnamese man rescued me and nursed me back to health." His throat tightened at the memory of his savior collapsing in the doorway of the hut when American soldiers arrived. The room began to spin and his pulse quickened at the vision of the women and children slaughtered by his own people. "No. I won't let it take me again," he protested, willing the images from his thoughts. His entire body shook.

"You returned to the states. Here, at the farm, remember?" Her hand cupped his cheek and he couldn't resist but to lean into it.

"Yes," he muttered. "But I was sick and had to go away."

Judy ran her thumb down his chin. "And you've been away ever since."

He nodded, unable to form words. All he could do was close his eyes and concentrate on the delicious touch of her skin on his.

"You're home, James."

A bolt of fear shot through him. "No, I'm not. I'm not staying." He jumped from the chair and moved away, leaving the comfort of Judy Gaylord. "You promised to show me where the documents are so I can leave. I've told you what you wanted to know. It's your turn."

Tears filled her eyes, but she stood and walked from the kitchen, pausing at the doorway. "Follow me. I'll show you where your mom hid the documentation. But you need to ask yourself why she left it here. Why didn't she take it to Miami when she moved there? Also, you could've had Cathy or Eric look for the documents, but you didn't. Instead you made the trip from Miami to your childhood home you swore you'd never return to. So you need to ask yourself why you really came back."

Chapter Eleven

JUDY FOUGHT the desire to beg his forgiveness for her betrayal. But Cathy was right about one thing, this wasn't about her. Even if he never wanted to see her again, she still knew deep in her heart that he belonged in Sweetwater, on his farm.

"Watch out." James clutched her waist and lifted her to the next step. His strength awed her.

"Thanks. Is your leg okay?" Judy stalled for a moment, enjoying his hands on her, but he quickly pulled them away and gestured for her to continue the climb.

"Yep. It's already better. My pants, on the other hand, not so much. I'm afraid I didn't pack enough."

They reached his parents' old room and went to the closet.

"I already looked there. Nothing but moths and some old shoes." James chuckled. The first hint of any happiness spread through the room like the bright sunshine through the window then quickly faded.

She continued to the back of the closet.

"I told you there isn't anything—"

She hit the wall with the side of her fist and the hidden door popped open.

"What the? I didn't know that was there. How did you?"

"Your mother. The week before you were due home, she brought me up here to show me something she wanted me to wear at our wedding." Her voice broke. "A family heirloom she kept hidden in here. She told me it was her secret hiding place. Not even your dad knew about it."

James gazed at her for a moment. "She loved you like a daughter. For years, she sent me pictures of you and your family."

Judy leaned her head against the wall, fighting the grief that still felt raw.

"What is it?" James asked.

"I lost her love. She hated me. You hated me. I was so selfish in my grief."

A hand, *his* hand, squeezed her shoulder. "She didn't. I don't."

Judy dug deep to keep the tears from flowing. "Thanks, but I know it's true. I would've clawed the girl's eyes out if things had been reversed."

"Oh, don't get me wrong. I wanted to string my cousin up by his toes and beat him like a piñata at a Fourth of July picnic, but by the time I left the hospital you both were happy. Knowing how unstable I was, I wasn't about to return and ruin it for you both."

She reached into the opening and pulled out some documents, stalling to pull herself together before facing him again.

"Eric's a good boy. He reminds me of Michael. He was a good man. I'm sorry for your loss." James toed the floor.

Judy handed him a stack then retrieved another. "Thank you. He *was* a good man." Her heart fluttered at the memory. "He did the right thing, even at a great cost."

James grunted and headed back into the bedroom, dropping the papers onto the bed. "Geesh, she kept a lot in there. Sometimes I think she never left this place. She gave up so many years of her life to be near me." His gaze wandered around the room before he lowered it to the pages in front of him. "They'll probably tear this place down and build some shopping mall on the property, or some garbage like that."

Judy sat on the other side of the bed and rummaged through the first few envelopes filled with old news clippings of James making the winning goal in a soccer game as a child, taking the little league team to the championship games in Knoxville. "Probably. I'd love to buy the old place, but it would be too big for me to live here alone. Besides, most of my money is invested in the shop. We're doing great, but it'll be awhile until I can recoup it all."

"You've done well." James snagged the news clipping from her grasp. "Hey, what's that? Wow, she kept this?"

"She kept everything about you. Look at this one."

He leaned into her, his closeness making it difficult to breathe. "That's from when I won my sixth grade spelling bee. You'd have thought I'd become president."

"I remember that. I was jealous because you beat me. It was the first time I noticed you." Judy flushed. "I mean—"

"You wore a yellow dress with daisies and a white hair tie." He smiled.

"Oh, you have a great memory."

"About certain things, yes."

Certain things? What did that mean?

Dang it, she felt like that little girl in sixth grade, making mooneyes at him. She straightened and moved to the next large manila envelope. Inside was a letter addressed to her. "What's this?"

"That's Mother's handwriting."

"I know, but what's it for? Why is it in here?"

James' shoulder nudged hers. "You could open it and find out."

His mischievous smile filled her heart with hope that he was okay and just didn't realize it yet.

"Right. Well, here it goes." She slid her finger under the lip and pulled a folded piece of yellowed paper out.

"I need my reading glasses." Judy lowered her feet to the floor to go retrieve her purse, but James' fingers wrapped around her arm.

"Here, use mine." He stood, removed a glass case from his pocket and handed it to her before returning to his seat. A little closer to her than before.

She lifted the glasses to her eyes, amazed she could see clearly. "Perfect, thanks."

Opening the letter, she discovered a full page of beautiful script.

Dear Judy, Martha's voice echoed in her head as she read.

"Read it out loud."

"Out loud?"

James smiled, revealing his perfect teeth. "Yeah, you have my glasses, remember?"

"Right." She nestled back against the headboard to brace herself from falling over.

"Dear Judy, You have and always will be my daughter. Every time I cross paths with you in town, my heart bleeds to reconnect. My only consolation for being apart from you is that I believe you and Michael are happy. That son of yours is becoming a fine young man. I've been proud of you both from a distance.

"Sending you away, and telling you I hated you, was the most difficult thing I've ever done. I hope you can find it in your heart to forgive the lie we've lived with all these years, but as a mother of a son, I'm sure you can understand. If Eric ever suffered the way my James has, you'd do anything to help him. Deep in my heart, I know you and my son belonged together, but life got in the way.

"Now, that my husband has passed, I'm leaving my home and the lies behind to be closer to James. I'm hoping to convince him to return home, to tell you the truth and start living again, but if you are reading this I failed and I'm gone now.

"I want you to have my grandmother's sapphire earrings, the ones you were to wear at your wedding to James. They've been kept for you all these

years as I've always wanted to pass them down to my daughter-in-law to keep in the family. I hope you treasure them despite how you feel about me.

"*With all my heart and love, Martha*"

Tears streamed down Judy's face, falling on the bottom of the paper. "She still loved me, even after what I did."

James brushed a wayward tear from her cheek. "Of course she did. Please don't blame her. All of this was my fault."

Judy rested the paper on her lap. "No, it's no one's fault. It was an ugly time. A tragic time, many died. Others came home broken. You weren't the only one. None of this is your fault."

"I was too weak." He bowed his head, his hands beginning to tremble again.

"No. Don't say that. You were—are strong. Look at what you've accomplished in life. You're a well-respected doctor, dedicating your life to helping others."

"Yes, everyone but my own mother. She left this house to be with me in hopes of returning someday. That never happened. She died in Miami." James rose from the bed, gesturing to the walls and windows around them. "And look what happened. Her home, our home, is now in ruin."

Judy sat up on her knees and caught his gaze. "No, it's not. Yes, there's some work to be done, but it can be repaired. Just like the souls of your patients can be repaired."

James raked his fingers through his silver flattop and toed a broken door handle left on the floor. "No, it's best to sell it. I had my chance to return and I didn't. It's time for me to find the document and head back to Miami. To dedicate my remaining days to helping veterans."

Judy spotted an envelope labeled *important documents* in the stack beside her. "You can't save them, you know. It's too late. It's time for you to stop punishing yourself."

James' brow furrowed. "What do you mean? I can help the veterans at the hospital."

Judy bit her bottom lip, unsure if she should push, but if now was all she had, push she would. "Not them. The men back in that foxhole, your friends. They died. You can't bring them back, but it wasn't your fault. You're not honoring their memory by hiding from life. They'd want you to—"

"Enough!" James snapped before he clutched his hands to both sides of his head, his face turning as red as leaves in autumn. "You don't know what you're talking about." Slowly, he lowered his hands and straightened. "I'm sorry. I didn't mean to be rude. But I haven't seen you since we were teenagers, you don't know me. I can't live here. This is a place I meant to never return to."

She stood, dropped the manila envelope on the bed and stared him down. "I won't beg you to stay, lie or cheat to keep you here. There's been enough of that. If you want to leave then here you go. You have your precious document, so go. But think about one thing. This house. Your mother's house. Is this how you want to leave it?"

Chapter Twelve

THE NIGHT CREPT BY, a distant owl hooting its presence each time James awoke. Dreams of Judy and him living in Sweetwater County—raising their children, farming their land—faded into a distant memory as he rose, dressed, and waited for Eric's arrival.

Judy's bright eyes and infectious smile pushed him through the darker moments of the night. Was it all a dream, or did she really appear before him yesterday wanting to help. He inwardly chastised himself for his uncivil behavior. It was tough to see her again, to keep his distance when she only sat an arm's length away.

Shaking his head of the visions of her beauty, he watched a bird swoop down and snag a worm from the front flowerbed, the garden that had once housed rose bushes and herbs, a color-infused welcome to all that came to their door. Now, only dirt, sticks, and rocks remained. All the tender loving care his mother had put into this home had vanished. His chest tightened at the thought of someone tearing down the home after it had been in his family for so many years. He'd failed his comrades during the war, his mother, and Judy. Could he fail centuries of family ancestry, too? Was Judy right? Did he owe it to his family to restore this house to its former glory?

Eric's car barreled down the gravel drive, sending a white cloud of dust behind him. Perhaps he could clarify what was to be done with the home once he signed the paperwork to sell it to the county.

Maybe it could be a home for children without parents. His mother would have loved that.

James rose and hopped off the second step at the sound of Eric's car door slamming. "Good morning, kid. Thanks for coming out so early."

"Not like you could walk into town, Old Man." Eric winked. "Got the documents?"

James nodded. "Sure do, but I have a question first."

"What's that?"

"You say the county wants this place. What for?" James held his breath.

"I guess they want to have the land."

James crossed his arms. "You mean they want to tear it down?"

Eric nodded. "I believe so. Why? You said you didn't care what happened to it, so we didn't look at contesting anything."

"I know. It's just that, this was my mother's home. Actually, it's been in my family for generations. In fact, I believe it was my great-grandfather who built the main building with his own two hands.

"Is that so?" Eric asked.

"Yes, so you can see why I'd prefer they didn't tear it down."

Eric scrubbed his jaw. "This complicates things. I'm not sure what the land was slated to be used for. If you decide not to take the deal, I can't promise you'll get another offer at the same price point."

James let out a loud exhale. "I see. Well, here are the documents, but can you give me a day to think about things? My flight leaves tomorrow, so that'll give me some more time."

He needed to talk about this with someone. Figure out what he should do, but who? Cathy? No. She'd just tell him to stay and she'd be moved in with him by the end of the week. It had to be someone who knew his mother and her wishes. Could he really speak to Judy about this? After all he'd said to her last night, would she even want to speak to him?

"Um...do you think your mother is busy?"

Eric shook his head. "No. Actually, I think she's just doing some cleaning at the shop this morning. Lisa wanted me to head over and check on her. I promised I would. It was the only way I could keep her from going to help clean, and with her pregnancy complications I don't want to take that chance."

"I wasn't aware."

Eric took the manila envelope and held it under his arm. "It's okay. It's just that she lost one of the babies early on." The man's lips curved downward, telling James he'd suffered a great loss.

"That's terrible. I'm so sorry."

"It's okay. I'm just thankful Lisa is doing so well now. We're keeping our fingers crossed she'll go full term. That's part of the reason for the quick marriage. I want my name on that birth certificate and I'm not taking any chances that her ex is going to show up and ruin everything."

James scratched his forehead.

Eric chuckled. "You didn't know that either? I'm shocked Cathy didn't spill it all to you already. The baby isn't mine biologically. Well, come on. I'll take you into town to see Mom."

"I didn't—"

Eric marched to his little, dark fancy car. "Yes, you did. Now, get in."

James' stomach rumbled so loud it echoed in the small space.

"You need food, too," Eric said.

"Good idea. I didn't feel much up to it last night."

Eric put the key in the ignition, but didn't start the car. "What happened last night?" he asked, his voice strained.

"I take it you've heard of my issues."

"I spoke with Cathy out of concern, but I'm asking you to clarify."

"I didn't hurt your mother."

Eric turned the key and the engine hummed. "I didn't think so, but I had to ask. Mom says you couldn't hurt her."

A strange flutter stirred in his belly. Dare he hope? "She should still stay away."

Eric turned onto the main road back to town. "Have you been violent in the last few years?"

"No."

"If there's one thing I know about my mother, she's not going to give up on you without more information. Mom's one determined woman. One with a strength that only compares to my Lisa. That's probably why I fell in love with her."

James eyed the hardware store at the edge of town. A *For Sale* sign hung in the window along with garden tools and cans of paint. Could he stay a little longer? Should he save his childhood home? "What if the house was fixed up? Would it sell then?"

"That's a question for a realtor. I will say that it's a buyer's market. Even if you sold the home, there's no guarantee the person won't flip it and resell the land."

James gnawed on his cuticle, a bad habit he'd tried to break but with little success. As they turned down Main, he spotted J and L Antiques. The door opened. His breath hitched and he leaned forward to catch a glimpse of Judy, but it wasn't her. He leaned back and found another cuticle to damage.

"Can I give you some advice?"

"Sure, kid. Why not?"

"You two need to talk. Not so much about what happened, but about your life since. Find out how each other lived. Only then can you both find closure...that's what I think, anyway."

James chuckled. "You came up with that all on your own?"

Eric parked the car and turned off the engine. "No, that's all Lisa. She's been nudging me since you arrived...with a sledge hammer. I think she feels like she owes Mom a happily-ever-after since Mom helped her find hers."

James lowered his hand to his lap. "Why's that?"

Eric smiled. "Sounds like a great story for Mom to tell you."

James gripped the door handle and took a long breath. "You're coming in, right?"

"Yep. Don't worry, she has a loud bark but can be reasonable."

James sighed then shoved the door open and marched to J and L Antiques. The girl named Lisa was right. He needed to know more about Judy's life over the years, and he'd reassure her that his life in Miami was as he'd planned it. They'd part ways on good terms and all would be well.

Chapter Thirteen

JUDY PACED the showroom floor around an antique coffee table. "Oh, dear. This is bad," she muttered.

"What's wrong?" Eric said, startling her. She'd been so busy fretting she didn't even hear the door jingle.

"Oh, Eric. I'm so sorry. I—" She turned the corner and ran smack into something hard.

Strong arms steadied her. "Judy," James smiled down at her then let her go and stepped back. "What's your distress? I'm sure between us we can figure it out." While his words comforted her, she couldn't help feeling it was his Ph.D. talking.

"Oh, um. I didn't know you were coming." She shot a sideways glance at her son, who stood beaming next to the register. She took a deep breath to collect herself. "I'm not sure how...Poor Lisa's going to be so disappointed. The Barn, something happened and they just told me we can't have the wedding there. It's some sort of code violation, so all events have been suspended until further notice."

"But the wedding's in ten days. Certainly they can fix it by then." Eric said.

Lisa waddled out from the back kitchen. "They've canceled all the events for the next thirty days. They said we could take a chance, but not to count on it." She rubbed the mounting tension out of the back of her neck.

"With all these new buildings in the area, isn't there somewhere else you could have it?" James asked, his baritone voice filling the room and her soul.

"Not anything that nice," Lisa replied.

Eric sighed. "Well, I'm not waiting. Lisa could have the baby early. We'll have to get married at the courthouse and have a ceremony later."

"No. There has to be another option." Lisa paced back around the register. "We could have it at the park."

Eric's brow furrowed. "We could try, but it's the rainy season. It's been gorgeous for weeks, so we're due for a good storm."

"True." Judy leaned against the wall, tilting her head back. "We can't disappoint my soon-to-be daughter-in-law." She reached over and squeezed Lisa's hand. "You've had such a rough time. This was your chance to feel loved and wanted. I know having everyone in town at your wedding will make you feel like one of us for good."

"You might not have..." James said, so faint she could barely hear him.

"What?"

James cleared his throat. "I'm saying you could have the wedding at the farm."

She lifted her head. Was he serious? The place was a disaster.

He held up a hand. "Hear me out. I want to put some money into fixing it up. I'm sure we can hire contractors on short notice, and if this is still the same Sweetwater County that I grew up in, Creekside, as well as the surrounding towns, will chip in to help pull off the wedding."

A warm tingle spread across her skin. "Are you saying you're going to stay?"

James scratched his forehead. "No, but I can't just watch the house my mother loved so much be torn down. It's the least I can do to honor her memory. Perhaps if we have the wedding there, some nice couple with a family will see how lovely it is. I don't care how much it sells for. I have more money than I know what to do with at this point in my life. I'll sell it for less to a family that can appreciate it."

"It might work." Eric slipped his cell phone from his pocket. "I can call in a few favors. I just helped settle a suit for the owner of an independent horticulture company. I'm sure they can help with the landscaping."

"So, when it's done you'll leave?"

James nodded. "It's for the best."

Eric patted her shoulder then offered his hand to James. "Thank you." They shook on the promise to hold a wedding at a dilapidated, old farmhouse, so that he could sell it and leave. "I appreciate this, old man."

"It's nothing, kid."

Her heart raced, and she struggled between being happy about him staying for at least a little while longer, and the fear of having to work with him on a wedding. The hole in her heart from their lost wedding still stung. It wasn't about her, though. This was for Lisa.

James stepped around Eric and stood a foot in front of Judy. "I'll only do this if it's okay with you."

She lifted her chin and plastered on a fake smile she hoped concealed her heartbreak. "Of course. It's kind of you to make such a sacrifice. It'll certainly take a lot of work, not to mention you won't be able to return home tomorrow. Will that be okay?"

"Okay? Heck, they've been after me to take vacation."

"Some vacation," she chuckled. "You'll be dirty, tired and probably do a lot worse to your body than that leg wound."

James winked. "I'm tough. I can handle it."

His long lashes drew her attention back to his bright, silver eyes. Eyes she could lose herself in for hours. She could do this. It would be fine. She just needed to stop looking at those eyes.

"Well, I guess we need to get to work then. I'll have to plan the wedding around the progress of the renovations. I can stage the main floor of the house with things from the shop. I'll have to come by and take measurements. I guess the first thing we need to do is give the house a good cleaning." She thought for a moment. "I'll call the Red Hat Society, they'll help."

James raised his thumb to his mouth then quickly dropped it to his side and toed the edge of the coffee table. "We're going to grab a bite to eat. You want to join us? We can plan while we fill our bellies."

"I'd love to, but I'm supposed to take Lisa to the dress-maker's."

Eric clapped his hands together once. "Great. We'll swing by there first, and then we can go."

Judy shook her head. "Most of the food's on Main right here. It seems senseless for you boys to drive us over and then back."

James cleared his throat. "It's no bother, and I'd love to get to know that special woman of yours for more than just a few awkward minutes." He smiled at Lisa then turned to the door.

"I think that's a great idea." Lisa took Eric's hand.

James looked at Judy then offered his arm.

She couldn't say no. Heck, she'd never been able to say no when he gave her that crooked smile. "Let me grab my purse."

Snatching it from behind the counter, she tripped over the taped cord running along the floor. She smoothed her skirt down and fluffed her hair before sliding her shaking hand into James' arm. "Eric, you better fix that before Lisa trips."

"Yes, Mother," he said, his voice filled with sarcasm.

They reached Eric's car, and James jumped in front of her, opened the door then stood back.

It had been a long time since a gentleman opened a door for her, excluding her son. Of course, he knew she'd knock him upside the head if he didn't. She sunk into the seat and pulled her feet in as gracefully as possible before the door closed. Lisa settled in the front passenger's seat while James came around the car and sat by her side. The motor hummed to life. She clutched her purse tight to her chest.

Eric put his hand on the passenger seat and looked out the back window to back out of the parking space. He mouthed, "It's okay."

She smiled and released her death grip. "I just want everything to be perfect for you two, that's all." No way would she admit that the man sitting beside her caused her entire body to feel like some freshman girl, in heat for the senior captain of the football team. With one wink, he'd turned her world upside down.

How ridiculous. She had a son, been married, not to mention she owned her own business. How hard could this be?

Taking a deep breath, she reassured herself there'd be no more nonsense over some man that couldn't wait to leave Sweetwater.

"Thanks for offering to help with the house." James' hand covered her shoulder and, with that one touch, her resolve crumbled.

Chapter Fourteen

How could I be such a clumsy fool? James wiped his sweaty palms down the sides of his pants. That woman turned him all around inside. What was he thinking inviting her to work on the house with him? They'd be in small areas, working together for ten days. His mouth had betrayed his will and now, he couldn't take it back.

All the nervous energy he felt around Judy worried him, but so far, he hadn't experienced any anxiety. In a way, the nervousness excited him instead of scaring him. Something about that woman always made everything better.

They climbed the steps to a Victorian style home with a wide wraparound porch. Flowers sprung to life from hanging baskets, and a dog barked in the distance. The house wasn't modest by any means, but still possessed southern charm. He remembered this home. Not that he'd ever been in it. During his youth, the mayor had lived there, and James' parents hadn't hung in those circles.

Eric pressed the bell, and it chimed in a pleasant melody, reminding him of classical music. The door swung open. Cathy stood there with straight pins through her shirt, some cloth mound with pins sticking out of it around her wrist and thimble on the end of her finger. "You're welcome to come in as long as Judy promises not to kill me."

"This is for Lisa. I'll be civil." Her words sounded forced and harsh, even to her own ears.

James had only heard her speak like that when she'd caught him smoking behind the bleachers his senior year. She'd called him an ashtray mouth that wasn't worth kissing. He pressed his hand to his mouth, stifling his laugh.

Judy shot him a sideways glance as if to tell him, *you best not be enjoying this*. He snagged her hand to keep her on the porch, waving Cathy to shut the door behind Eric. "Listen, she—"

"I said I'd play nice, now let's start helping Lisa."

"That's not it." James' fingers naturally entwined with hers, as if they remembered their place in life. "Cathy isn't at fault here. My mother swore her to secrecy, guilted her into keeping our secret. She said some awful things to Cathy that she later regretted, but she knew it was necessary. Cathy's a victim in all this, not the instigator."

"Did he know?" Judy didn't look at him, only averted her gaze to the porch swing.

"Who?" He tightened his grip, nudging her to face him. When she did, he saw the tears welling in her eyes and it broke his heart.

"My husband. Did Michael know you were alive?"

James could only shake his head. Did she think everyone in town knew but her? "No. He never knew," he replied softly. "Mother told me he'd tried to apologize to her while I was in the hospital. She asked him, if I was alive would he step aside. This was after Eric was born, and my mother said Michael's eyes were large pools of sadness. At first, she wasn't sure if he was upset over the loss of his cousin or the thought of losing you. When he finally spoke, he told her that he'd grown to love you in a way he never knew possible, but that if I was alive, he'd only want your happiness. That he'd step aside."

Her hand fluttered to her chest. She blinked back the tears and straightened. He wanted to pull her into his arms and make all the pain vanish from her life.

"Well, that's good to know. Thank you." She lifted her chin and smiled. "We better go in."

His fingers protested at the loss of her touch, but he let her go and opened the door. A living room off the foyer was full of fabric and craziness. A young woman, with long legs and a beautiful smile, stood on a pedestal, pale pink cloth wrapped around her body.

"I thought you decided to go with white," Judy asked.

Lisa shook her head. "I only said that in hopes you might let me borrow your amazing dress, but after speaking to Cathy, it's just not possible. There isn't enough material to cover this belly."

"Oh, that's sweet, dear. But as much as I'd love for you to wear that dress, I don't think it was ever meant to be worn. I'd be worried I was cursing you somehow." Judy lifted a magenta roll of fabric. "Is this what I'll be wearing?"

Lisa wavered, but quickly recovered her balance. "When I thought I was wearing white. Now, I think we'll go with more pastel colors. If that's okay with you."

Cathy grabbed a tape measure from the table. "You men need to leave. We'll be talking dress styles and no groom should see the dress before the wedding."

Eric stood and kissed Lisa's hands. "You'll be beautiful, no matter what you wear."

"Sweet. Now out, or I'll start pinning you instead of the fabric," Cathy scolded.

"Come on, old man. We should go in the other room."

"You sure you can make a dress in under two weeks? I mean, that's a lot to ask," Lisa said.

"Oh darling, I made two prom dresses in less than that time, sequins and all."

Judy sat in an antique claw-foot chair. "She did."

James halted in the doorway. Images flashed...her emerald dress, with the spaghetti straps, her auburn hair twisted up on her head, showing off her slender, kissable shoulders. "And they were beautiful," he said. "They were both the belles of the ball."

Then he retreated from the room before he could embarrass himself any further. What the hell was he doing?

Eric elbowed him in the side. "Nice move."

"What are you talking about?" he barked before finding a seat at the kitchen table.

"You, flirting. Mom told me you were suave."

"Flirt? Me? I don't flirt."

"Sure." Eric rolled his eyes. "Just like you don't still having feelings for my mother." He sauntered over and opened the refrigerator before James had a chance to protest. "I realize you've got some years on me." Eric handed him a cold beer then sat across the table from him. "But can I give you some advice?"

"What's that?" James twisted the top off and tossed it in the trash can near the wall.

"Why not get to know her again?"

Now, it was his turn to roll his eyes. "Not that again."

"Just hear me out. It can be as friends if that's what you'd prefer. But I think you owe this to her. After all these years, she has a right to have a chance to digest all of this. She has questions, and you're the only one with the answers."

James gripped the bottle. "I'm done talking about the war."

Eric set his beer on the table and leaned forward. "I'm not talking about the war. She just wants to know who you are now. If you've had a good life. If you still hate lima beans. Just give her a chance to adjust to you being alive before you flee again. Close a few doors and open a new one if that's what's meant to be."

James stared past him and picked at the label on the bottle. Could he really have a second chance to know her? Was it right, knowing he could never be with her? He'd learned a long time ago that he didn't deserve the white picket fence kind of life. Would she understand that?

"I guess I could talk to her," James said slowly. "It seems like we'll have plenty of time. But at the end of the two weeks, I'll be gone. Nothing will keep me here. It's best for this town that I return to Miami, and that's what I'm going to do."

Chapter Fifteen

THE THOUGHT of having something to organize and focus on, a project of sorts, soothed Judy for the first time in days.

"The dress will be beautiful, don't worry." She clutched Lisa's shoulder and pulled her to her side as they walked into the Southern Style Café.

"Thanks. I wish I could wait until we had the baby—"

"No way. Not happening." Eric took her hand, kissed her cheek then whispered something that made her blush.

"Okay, we won't wait." Lisa carefully lowered to the booth and slid in, Eric taking the seat next to her. Leaving Judy with James.

That unwelcomed flutter in her belly returned. Calming herself, she picked up a menu, despite the fact that she knew everything on it by heart. "Whatcha gettin'?"

Lisa sighed. "A char-grilled chicken salad. I'll swell even more if I have something salty, like French fries.

Judy dropped the menu back behind the napkin dispenser. "Sounds good to me." Hearing a buzz, she retrieved her cell phone from her purse. "Oh, good. The Red Hat Society will be at your house, James, at eight in the morning to start scrubbing it down. You should have contractors coming in on Wednesday, leaving us

Thursday and Friday to fix anything left that we can do ourselves. Saturday and Sunday we'll do the painting. Oh, you'll need to meet me at the paint shop to pick out colors. We need to *at least* have the main floor done. I've got Pete's Window Washers coming at eight in the morning on Tuesday next week, and the movers will transport furniture from the shop on Thursday. We'll do the staging Friday and have the wedding Saturday afternoon."

James whistled. "How did you possibly work all that out already?"

Lisa laughed then grasped her belly and moaned. "Oh, you don't know Judy. No one has a prayer at keeping up with her. The woman's made of pure adrenaline."

Eric nodded. "And tough as nails."

Judy slid the stylus from the bottom of her phone. "Okay, dress? Check. Venue? Check. Eric's handling the grounds. I'll handle the staging. James, you'll need to call the contractors this afternoon. Tell the owner at Bellings Construction that he better make this a priority, or I'll have to call his ex-wife."

James shook his head. "I don't want to blackmail someone."

Judy cocked her head to the side. "Do I look like a woman that blackmails people? Heck, you don't know me at all, James Benjamin."

"No, you're right. I don't...not anymore. But I think it's time I change that."

Judy scribbled nonsense on her phone despite her trembling hand. Did she really hear that right? She turned and opened her mouth to speak but nothing came out.

James lifted his hand and waved a waitress over. "I think it's time to order."

"You okay over there, Mom? I've never seen you so quiet before." Eric and Lisa both lifted their menus up so their faces were covered. They were up to something.

James set his menu on the table. "Leave your mother alone, children." They all burst out laughing.

She stared at them, dumbfounded. She was sitting at a mental table.

James nudged his shoulder into hers. "It was funny."

Thank the Lord, Judy thought as the waitress approached. Unfortunately, the woman just stood there, staring between her family and James as they continued their ruckus. Judy knew the gal, but couldn't recall her name since she lived a few towns over.

Lisa dabbed at her eyes. "Don't worry. We're okay, really."

"Um, sure," the waitress said. "What can I get you?"

Eric set his menu down. "Three grilled chicken salads and water with lemon."

James clasped his hands together in front of him. "Make that four."

"Sure.."

"Is this where you guys usually eat lunch?" James moved his arms to his lap, allowing another server to place waters.

"Sometimes," Eric answered. "There's a good sandwich shop around the corner, too."

Lisa sipped her water. "Yeah, but Judy lives at the coffee shop. She's gotta have her London Fog fix."

Judy dabbed at the water droplets on her cup. "You're just jealous because you had to switch to decaf."

"That explains a lot," James said.

Judy twirled her straw, moving the ice around. "Explains what?"

"In a matter of an hour, you've organized a wedding, a refurbishment of an old farmhouse, and staging. Not to mention had a dress fitting. Woman, you haven't slowed down one bit, you know?" James leaned over the table as if to whisper some secret. "She was captain of the girls volleyball team, prom queen, lead in the school play and still managed to hold down a job and make straight A's. And that was all in one semester."

Judy smacked his arm. "You exaggerate."

"Do I?" James' eyebrows rose. "Should I mention you were

also editor of the school newspaper? Led a drive to collect food for the homeless, single-handedly ending world hunger?"

"See, you're wrong. I was only the assistant editor."

James put his hand to his mouth. "Oh, no. You were such a failure."

"I see you haven't changed either. You still tease people mercilessly."

Lisa tapped the end of her knife to the table. "Hey, you two, break it up. The food's here."

James smiled as he ate, showing a carefree side of him she hadn't seen since his arrival. The side that always made her laugh and feel full of life.

They chatted about Creekside and who was who while they ate, as if they'd been warped back to 1970 and they were on a Friday night date. Except it wasn't forty plus years ago, and this wasn't a date.

Eric spoke about local businesses, economy, and politics, while Lisa chimed in about some of her views. Before Judy realized it, the café had emptied out and the sun was setting. "Where did the time go? Oh no, Bellings Construction will be closed. You'll have to call them first thing in the morning."

James folded his napkin and placed it on the table. "Don't worry. I can take care of one thing on that list of yours."

Judy sauntered out the door and eyed her car in front of her store a few doors down. Conflicted, she looked back at James, and her legs froze as if her body protested leaving the man behind.

"Sorry, but I'm exhausted. You know, working for two right now and all." Lisa smiled and Eric reached over, covering her belly with his hands.

"We should get you home, sunshine." Eric insisted on paying the bill, and they all left the restaurant. "I've got to run to the office for a bit. Would you mind giving Lisa a ride, Mom? I'll come by to check on you in a couple hours." Eric bent over and spoke to Lisa's growing belly. "You too, Princess Amelia." Then he kissed her belly, and Judy felt warm all over. Seeing her son happy, happier than she'd ever seen him, made her believe anything was possible in this world.

Lisa took James' hands. "Thank you so much. We really appreciate you offering your home for our wedding. It's a beautiful piece of countryside, and I couldn't think of a more amazing place to have the ceremony and reception."

"Hey, it's an excuse to fix my house up to sell, so I should thank you."

Lisa leaned in and whispered something to him before taking Judy's hand and ushering her away.

"You'll be at the farm tomorrow morning. Right, Judy?" James called.

"I'll be there," she yelled back, before turning back to Lisa. "What did you whisper to him?"

Lisa smiled in that mischievous way she'd perfected. "That we both knew why he really wanted to help with the wedding."

Chapter Sixteen

SUNLIGHT FILTERED through the dirty glass of the attic room window, announcing the morning. With one short stretch, James jumped to his feet. The night had been free of terrors, allowing sleep to invigorate him for the first time in ages. He had to face the typhoon of activity that would no doubt ensue with Judy's entrance, after all.

He couldn't recall the last time he'd enjoyed an evening out with friends. Heck, he couldn't remember the last time he went out with friends. Colleagues, sure. But friends?

He quickly showered, shaved and put on the fresh pair of pants he made Eric stop to purchase last night, along with the blue shirt.

A knock sounded at the door, so he grabbed his work boots, also purchased last night, and took the stairs two at a time, jumping the broken one. His joints didn't feel the pressure of age after a great night's sleep. "Coming!"

Opening the door, he found Judy with a bag and a paint wheel. She was dressed in jeans, a light green sweater and her smile. Her gaze filtered down his clothes.

"I thought I needed some new digs if I was going to remain

for two weeks. Eric took me by a store last night. Nothing fancy, but—"

"It looks good. Blue's my favorite color." Her smile widened.

"I remember."

An awkward silence followed, making him shift between his feet.

"Well, are you going to invite me inside, or should we conduct business out here?"

He stepped out of the way. "Come in. It's pretty shabby, but I'm sure when you're done the place will sparkle."

"Well, that's the plan." Judy sauntered into the kitchen, her familiar,fI graceful walk begging him to follow. "I'd like to run a suggestion by you about color if you're open to it."

"Sure. But I'll be honest. Home décor isn't my strong suit." He chuckled.

Scattering her stuff all over the table, she picked up the color wheel and held it to the wall. "I'm thinking about staying with your mother's old colors. She had fantastic taste. We can go for a country-chic kind of feel with a little modern bling for accents. Her color pallet was perfect for this house." She paused and lowered the color wheel, her eyes downcast.

"What is it?"

"I'd like to honor her with this remodel. I, um...loved your mother and never had a chance to, well...you know."

He wanted to comfort her, but something held him back. Instead of pulling her into his arms, he only rubbed her shoulder. "I think that's a terrific idea. Kind of what I was hoping for myself."

She swiveled away and grabbed her cell phone. "Great, I'll match the colors and order the paint."

"Have I thanked you for doing this yet?" He longed to tell her how amazing she was, that he'd never stopped thinking of her, but he couldn't form the words. Why? Fear? "Mother loved you, too. She spoke of you often, right up until the day she died."

Judy's face lit up, but tears filled her eyes. "Really? Did she ever truly forgive me?"

"According to her there was never anything to forgive. That's why she had to leave. The lie became too much for her. Looking back, the lie was too much for all of us."

"Then why'd you keep it? Why not tell me the truth years ago?"

"I was scared."

"Of what?"

James lifted his hand to his mouth, but forced it back to his side. "At first...of hurting you, then of letting you down. I wasn't the man you once loved. That and you had a family."

"I understand, but why not later? I mourned you. We, Michael and I, mourned you every day. He would have loved to have seen you again."

"I was selfish." James fought to keep control of his voice as it threatened to crack. "I-I didn't think I had the strength to see you with him."

"Oh." Judy lifted the color pallet and her phone and headed to the next room. "I'm sorry. For many things."

The mood in the room had darkened so quickly. He longed for the happiness he felt the night before. To hear her laughter and see her smile. "Can we make a deal, if we're going to spend the next nine or so days together?" Though she still faced away from him, he noticed her hand move to her face.

"Depends," Judy said. "Your mother taught me never to enter into an agreement without knowing all the facts."

"She was a smart lady." He steadied his hands and forced his emotions down. Taking her arm, he turned her to face him. "Let's try to forget the past and enjoy the moment. I don't want to make you unhappy. It's part of the reason I never came back. To know I caused you so much pain..." His voice betrayed him, but he had to force the words out. "Now I have the chance to make up for past sins."

"I don't know if I can forget, but I'll try."

"Well, a wise woman once told me to forgive is easier than to forget. So, can you forgive me?"

Judy squeezed his hand, but averted her gaze. "Forgive you? What for?"

"For breaking a promise." He tilted her chin up so she'd look at him. "I promised to return to you no matter what, but I didn't."

"But you were injured, and then I—"

"Things happened. We've learned a lot in our lives. I don't know about you, but I'd much rather part as friends and live the remainder of my days in peace. You might not ever forget my failures, but I hope you'll find it in your heart to forgive me."

"Of course I forgive you, but how can you ever forgive me?"

He smiled. "That's not the hard part. It's forgiving ourselves that'll be the challenge." The fresh floral smell of her perfume beckoned him closer but all he could manage was to close his eyes and lean his head against hers.

The crackle of gravel under tires drew his attention to the window. He stepped back, peering through the windows to find the women from the Red Hat Society barreling down his drive in a long caravan. Taking a long draw of the floral scent, he held it into his lungs before backing away from her. "It looks like it's time to start."

Judy straightened her sweater and retreated to the kitchen, only to reappear at their guests' arrival on the front steps with no trace of tears. "Ladies, thank you so much for coming."

"Hi, James," Cathy greeted him with a quick hug.

"Cathy?" Judy said harshly. "You didn't have to come. I mean, your talents are needed for sewing the dresses."

Cathy smiled, the sweet, Southern belle charm nearly bowling him over. "No need to worry. Both dresses will be ready. I want to offer my talents in other areas."

"I bet you do," Judy muttered under her breath before taking a broom from one of the other ladies and handing it to her. "Then let's get started."

James watched as the ladies stood there in a stare down. This wasn't going to end well. "I'll move the few pieces of furniture out of the way. Judy, perhaps you can help me in the kitchen." He walked between them, prying the mop from Judy's hands. Best she remain unarmed. "Cathy, do you think you can start in the front room?"

"We'll head upstairs." Two ladies smiled and scurried by him, obviously retreating to safer ground.

Another lady stepped forward. "It's nice to have you back, James. I'm Connie, Eric's assistant. I went to school with you."

"Yes, I remember. It's a pleasure, and thank you for your help." He offered his hand.

"I love the idea of restoring this house," Connie said, glancing around. "It's my favorite in the entire county."

"Perhaps I should hire you as my realtor?" James teased.

"Not me, but I know several. Judy already told me to have them come out a week from Friday for a walk through."

"She did?" He heard the disappointment in his own voice, but why? It was what he wanted, wasn't it?

"Yes. That is what you were hoping for, right?" Connie asked, concern etched on her face.

Cathy scooted closer and leaned in. "So he thinks. Men are a little slow, though." She disappeared to the front room before he could question her. The woman had a way of stirring up trouble, always with the best intentions, though.

"Yes, that's the plan."

"Well, if something changes let me know. I best be getting to work, or there won't be anything to show."

"Be careful of the second step," James warned, and offered his hand to help her over.

"Still the same gentleman, I see." She winked before trudging up the rest of the stairs with a mop and bucket in one hand.

The ladies worked more efficiently than bees in a hive. Years of dust and dirt were swept, vacuumed and wiped away in a matter of hours. After scrubbing out the refrigerator, cabinets, and pantry, Judy set to work on the kitchen table.

"I think we should refinish this," she said. "I'll get some stain if you'd like. Can you sand it down this evening?"

"Sure. I just need to find the sander."

She smiled. "Looks like we'll be pulling an all-nighter. We need to go through all those boxes, too. There might be some accent pieces we can utilize."

"That's a big job. Should we ask some of the ladies to stay? Cathy—"

"They've worked hard enough," Judy said. "I don't want to ask too much of them. As for Cathy, she needs to finish those dresses."

James covered her hand to stop her vicious scrubbing. "Hey, what did that table ever do to you?"

"I need to scrub it clean."

"No, you want to take your anger out on it. We made a promise, remember? You said you'd forgive me."

Swiping a stray hair from her face, she sat down in one of the chairs. "It's not you."

He'd always known that forcing Cathy to keep his secret would be a strain, but now that it was all in the open, Judy would of course blame her for the deception. "It's Cathy. I know she can be a handful, but you two were so close back in high school. What happened?"

"You know what happened." Judy bit her bottom lip. "My best friend in the entire world treated me like garbage when I needed her most. Then I find out she kept a secret from me, one that could've changed my life."

"It wasn't her fault." James sunk into the chair next to her. "I never realized how many people would be affected by my lie. I thought I'd already been forgotten by the time I returned home. This is on me, not Cathy."

"You might have made her promise to keep the secret, but she still had a choice. I was her best friend." She stood and threw the towel down on the table. Pacing around the room, she huffed, "She knew all these years, even after Michael died, yet she never told me. I had a right to know. She accuses me of being selfish, but I think she was the one that was selfish. She hoped all these years she'd keep you for herself. You knew she had a crush on you."

"Judy. She was married and had children. Never once did we see each other. I don't believe—"

"Well, I do. That woman accused me of being selfish, and for a moment I believed her, but it's not about that. It's about my right to know the truth, to make informed decisions in my life. She's the one who's selfish. It tore her up that you and I were together, and then she found a way to keep us apart."

"I'm done with the front room, bath, stairwell, and basement. I think it's best that I go home and work on those dresses now." Cathy's small lips were drawn into a thin, forced smile as she stepped through the doorway into the kitchen. Her shoulders slumped and her knuckles were blanched from her death grip on the broom.

Judy stopped dead in her tracks, her mouth hanging open and her eyes wide.

"I'll walk you out." James quickly ushered Cathy to the door before all-out war erupted. "Listen, I know Judy said some hateful things, but she doesn't mean it. I know she doesn't."

Cathy shook her head. "She does. I knew the price when I agreed to keep your secret, but I did it anyway. Not because of the reason she accuses me of, but because I couldn't bear to see my best friend face a decision I knew she couldn't make. Judy's always been about loyalty and honor. Would you have wanted her to divorce her husband, or have to make the choice to stay with him knowing you were alive? I didn't. Either way, she lost. The best scenario was for her to live happy, as life would allow. Perhaps I was wrong. Perhaps I should have told her, but it's too late now."

James followed her to a fancy sedan and opened her car door for her. "It's never too late."

"I know. That's why I'm here."

James stepped back. Was Judy onto something? Did Cathy still have feelings for him?

"Relax, I'm not talking about me. As the Southern saying goes, *men are dumb.*" She settled into the driver's seat then looked up at him. "You and Judy. It's time you kids were finally together, and I mean to see that happen." Cathy's mischievous grin reappeared. "Now, go back in there and woo that girl." She slammed the door then rolled the window down a crack.

James shook his head. "It's not like that. I'm leaving in less than two weeks. We just agreed to be friends."

Cathy started her engine. "You've been lying and hiding from the truth so long, you wouldn't know it if it bit you in the ass."

Her car took off, sending small pebbles into his shins. Dang, that woman was crazy. He wasn't living a lie anymore. He'd faced the truth by coming clean to Judy, Cathy, and the entire town. He'd faced his demons and was a better man for it. A darkness had lifted from his heart by facing it all, but he wouldn't risk her life. What if he had a nightmare or a flashback? No, it wasn't worth the risk.

He marched back up the porch, pushing Cathy's words from his mind. Judy sat on the porch swing, her head buried in her hands. He moved to her side, his heart aching to make her feel better, to make the pain of all this go away. He'd do anything. Move mountains, rebuild houses...was that what he was doing? Making her feel better? No, it was self-therapy, a way to honor his mother.

Stop lying to yourself, Cathy's words echoed in his head.

Oh, dear Lord, I'm in trouble.

Chapter Seventeen

Judy rocked in the swing, trying to find an escape. What was she doing? Her emotions were going batty, and that wasn't like her. It was time she put her big girl panties on and dealt with a few things. She shot up from the swing and smacked into James. He caught her around the waist before she fell back. How long had he been standing there?

"You okay?" His voice sounded raspy.

Had she disappointed him with her behavior? Heck, she'd disappointed herself. "I-I'm sorry I shot my mouth off. I don't know why I did that."

"I do." He tucked a bit of hair behind her ear. "As much as you try not to be, you're human."

She smacked his shoulder, trying to act playful, though she felt anything but. "What are you trying to say? Are you calling me an overachiever again?" She was an overachiever all right, at letting her emotions run away with her.

"No. I'm saying you don't have a dishonest bone in your body. You're one of the hardest working people I've ever known, and you can't stand idle gossip. You're everything Cathy isn't. *But* she is also loving, creative, and more loyal than you think. You expected her to tell you the truth no matter what because you believe that's what you would have done."

She opened her mouth to protest, but his fingers gently covered her lips. Fighting the urge not to kiss them, she turned her head.

"She acted with her heart, instead of loyalty. Those are two conflicting traits. You have no idea the battle she went through to decide right from wrong. While you're black and white, she's completely gray."

"Trying to shrink me, James?"

His eyebrows rose.

"It sounds like a Psych 101 lesson. Hope you can get a refund on that fancy degree of yours, because you're wrong. You see, I'm sitting in the gray area right now. My mind already understands that she did what she thought was best. She followed what you wanted, but that doesn't mean my emotions are in check."

"Ah, but that's for an entirely different reason." He smirked.

"If you're so smart, why can't I be in the same room with her and not want to pull out her over-permed hair?"

His lips curled into a mischievous smile. "That's a Psych 102 lesson. That'll cost you."

"Oh, really?" She folded her arms over her chest. "Okay, I'll bite. What'll it cost me?"

He stepped back and toed the splintered wood on the front porch. "You'll have to go to dinner with me Friday night. My treat, but you'll have to drive. I've called the rental place and they said I'd have to go to Nashville to get a car. I thought about it but figured I needed to stay around here for the contractors and such."

"James Benjamin, are you asking me out?" Judy lifted a hand to her chest, more to calm her thrashing heart than to feign shock, but he didn't need to know that.

"Well, how about a working dinner? You know, we'll turn it

into a shopping and eating trip in town. No offense, I like the kid and all, but I think I'd prefer to go furniture shopping with you."

"Kid?"

James chuckled. "Just some manly roaring contest. It's all in jest. No worries."

"Good. It means a lot that you've taken to Eric. He's had a rough time since his father passed away."

"He's always been a good kid. I know Michael was a proud father."

What? "How?"

"Mother kept me apprised. She'd share photos when she could pry one from a friend or neighbor without too many curious questions. She always kept a close eye on you guys, even if it was from afar."

Judy's chest tightened. "She was a remarkable woman."

"Yes, she was." He sighed. "I think she's smiling down on us right now, happy we're fixing up the family home."

Judy entwined her fingers between his. They fit perfectly, as if they instinctively remembered the exact contour of his hand. Which, of course, was crazy since their hands had changed over the years. She shook her head, chastising herself for acting like a lovesick teenager. The man made it clear he was returning home to Miami. Mending fences and fixing houses was all that was on his mind. Mending and fixing hearts was not.

James squeezed her hand. "What is it?"

"Nothing." She took a long breath. Should she tell him the old feelings were still there, or would she send him running back to Miami? Worse, would he tell her he forgave her, but could never feel anything for her again after what she did? "I'm glad I have this opportunity to sort of right some wrongs, that's all."

A large, white truck pulling into the drive broke the quiet moment, as did the flow of the Red Hat ladies leaving the house. Judy quickly stepped back and smoothed her hair.

"Thanks for the help, you two," Wanda, her old friend since high school mumbled.

"Sorry, we were working out a few details," Judy said.

Wanda winked. "I bet you were."

Judy felt her cheeks flush, and she grabbed a bucket from Wanda. "Let me carry this for you."

James took a few items as well, dropped them at the car, then went over to greet the contractor climbing out of the white truck. When the men exchanged a boisterous reunion, Judy realized she'd forgotten that Richard Bellings had gone to school with them.

"Good to see you," Richard said. "Wow, I can't believe you're alive.

Judy set the bucket down in the trunk of Wanda's sedan. "Thanks again, ladies. I greatly appreciate your help."

Wanda elbowed her in the side. "He's still a fox. Oh, and I heard he's unattached. You go, girl." She winked then climbed into the driver's seat and started the engine.

Judy felt her entire body flush. Hot flash. Yep, had to be. She should start getting those any day now. It had nothing to do with James.

Another woman hopped into the car then Wanda tore down the drive, leaving a dust trail in her wake.

Richard slapped James on the back. "Man, it's so good to see you. Last I saw you was when I'd returned home from basic and you were headed out. After all these years...wow. Well, tell me what I can do for y'all."

"We're fixing the old house up for a wedding and an eventual sale to some nice family," James said.

"What? You're not staying around here?"

Judy's insides rolled in an empty feeling, already knowing how he'd answer.

"Just for about two weeks, then I'll head back to Miami and my job."

Richard stared at him for a moment then noticed Judy still rooted to the driveway. "Hey, Judy. How you doing today? Looking good as always."

"Thanks, Richard," she managed, forcing her hand down from her quaking belly.

James stepped between them, a strange crease in his brow. "Yeah, well. This way. You got married and have a few kids, right?"

Richard's smile faded a bit as he lifted his hat and ran his hand through his sweaty hair. "Not any more. Kids moved away and wife left three years ago."

"Sorry to hear that." James opened the front door. "Okay, so there's some drywall repair needed there, and we'll have to check the foundation. See that crack near the ceiling?"

Richard held the door open for Judy.

"Hey, you need to write this down or something?" James asked.

"Oh, yeah. Right." Richard pulled a small notebook and pen from the front pocket of his shirt. "Looks like more than just drywall." He ran his hand over the far wall. "There's water damage."

"I fixed that already. Loose pipe upstairs. The master bath is right over us."

"Gotcha. Hopefully there isn't any rot."

Judy crossed the floor and pointed at the ceiling fan. "Could you remove this monstrosity? I'd prefer to replace it with a chandelier or antique light fixture."

"Of course, hon." Richard saddled up beside her.

"I can handle that," James said. "Let's keep you focused on the major repairs. Follow me."

Judy let the men roam the house to check on repairs while she retired to the boxes in the garage. One by one, she went through ten of them before deciding to take a break and move onto the furniture.

SPRING IN SWEETWATER COUNTY

Richard appeared in the kitchen just as she was struggling to tug an antique chair through the doorway. "Need some help?" he sauntered over, his thick arms making lifting the chair an easy feat.

"Wow, you're handy," Judy laughed.

"We're all done, so I'll see you soon," James said, standing with his arms folded across his chest.

Judy sat down in the antique chair, a cloud of dust poofing up around her. "Guess I'll be re-covering this. So, how long will it take to make all the repairs?" Judy asked.

Richard opened his notebook and did some figuring. "About a week."

Judy shot up from the chair. "A week?"

"Hey, there's a lot of work to do here."

Judy pressed her hands to her hips. "Richard Bellings, you've got two days. I don't care how many men it takes. Do you hear me?"

"For you, sugar, I'll do it in two, but you'll have to find some extra hands to help. I don't have enough men on staff to handle this size job in two days. I'll have the lumber and supplies dropped off tomorrow, and we'll start the work the next day." Richard leaned in. "You have a speck of dirt here." He brushed something from her forehead. "We'll make this work. You and me."

"I'll show you out." James turned on his heels and headed for the door.

"Guess I better be gettin'. Hope to see you soon." He winked. "Man, he's gotten grumpy over the years," he muttered before sauntering after James.

James returned a few minutes later. "Still as flirtatious as ever I see."

"What are you talking about?" Judy kicked a box out of the way and opened the next.

"Like you don't know. He's always had eyes for you."

Judy opened her mouth to protest, but James disappeared before she had a chance. Dang, that man was exhausting.

Chapter Eighteen

JAMES CHECKED his watch for the tenth time that morning. The sun was up and he wanted to go into town early and be back before Richard delivered the supplies. He rubbed the back of his neck, still sore from moving all the boxes. His fingers grazed the exact spot where Judy had massaged a kink out the night before. The hair on the back of his neck prickled at the memory. She still had magical hands, a breathtaking smile, and a beautiful soul.

Of course, he wasn't the only one who noticed. He stood and paced the front porch. Richard had put the moves on her in high school. Even back then, the man never sat right with him. Certainly, Judy saw past his flirtatious ways for who he really was. How he'd even maintained a marriage for as long as he had was beyond James' comprehension.

The night before he was supposed to leave for basic, he saw Richard manipulate Cathy into taking a walk alone. From what she said later, the man didn't understand the word *no*. Good thing Cathy had a great right hook. If James hadn't left for basic an hour after he found out, he would've punched the guy's lights out.

Nope, he had no business hanging around Judy, especially not alone.

Finally, Eric's car pulled to a stop in front of the house and James shook off his memories then jumped in the passenger seat. "Good morning."

"Good morning to you." Eric smiled. "I thought we'd stop at the coffee house on the way to the shop. Marcus ordered some caffeine free organic coffee and offered to make Lisa a latte this morning. I thought it would be great to surprise her with one."

"Sure. I'm more of a hot tea man myself, but sounds good."

The car rumbled down the drive, and Eric turned to head to town. "I heard you guys had a productive day yesterday."

"Yes, your mother's in total control."

Eric chuckled. "Oh, I'm sure. Lisa and I are thankful this project is distracting her."

"Why's that?"

Eric sighed. "Don't get me wrong. Lisa and I adore her...it's just that she needs things to focus on. And now that the business is running smoothly, she's been hovering over Lisa and the baby. Not to mention wanting to work constantly so Lisa will rest. My fiancé will go stir-crazy. As a matter of fact, I was hoping you'd get her out of the shop more." He glanced over at James. "Help a man out here, will you? I have a pregnant fiancé, with a mother hen. My life is going to get complicated."

James watched the town come into view. "I don't think I should get caught up in any family business."

"Oh, you won't." Eric pulled into a parking place three spaces down from the antique store and a few from the coffee shop.

People milled around out front, chatting. "I guess some things do change in a small town," James remarked as they stepped in line near the counter.

"Why do you say that?"

James eyed a couple huddled together in the corner, sipping from paper cups with plastic lids. "In my day, we used to hang out at the café. We'd share a shake and fries. Now it's all about the coffee."

Eric inched forward in line. "People still hang at the café in the afternoon and evening, but this is kind of the local spot for teens before school starts and where workers get their morning fix."

The man behind the register hit a few buttons then looked up at them. "Hey, man! Let me whip up that latte. You want anything else?"

"Hey, Marcus," Eric said. "Yes, I'd like a large black coffee to go, please. And anything James here wants."

"Hi there, Mr. B. It's a pleasure. I heard you were back in town. What can I get for you?"

"Um, a black hot tea." James caught whispering behind him and glanced back to see three women eyeing him from a few feet away.

"It must be tough feeling like a celebrity, but the people in this town really do care. Even if they have to talk it to death before they greet you." Marcus tossed his dark hair back from his eyes.

James pulled his wallet out. "It's my turn to pay, kid."

"You don't—"

"Don't argue with me. Trust me, I'll win."

Eric held up his hands in surrender and stepped to the end of the counter.

After paying, James stood next to the three women while willing his hot tea to appear faster. A tap on his shoulder warned a quick escape wasn't in the cards.

"Hi, James," one of the women said. "I'm not sure you remember me, but I was a year behind you in school. I cheered for the varsity team, though. I still remember that touchdown. The one in the final ten seconds of the game your senior year, when you—"

"He jumped over the entire defensive line and landed on his feet in the end zone," another woman with poofy hair finished.

James shifted between feet and eyed the counter. "Um, yes, I remember you both."

The women cackled like old hens in unison.

"Well, it's good to have you back in town. Don't be a stranger," the third woman said, with a little more dignity than the other two.

"Here you go," Marcus said, leaning over the counter. "One organic decaf latte, one black coffee, a hot tea, and one London Fog on the house for Mrs. G. You don't mind taking it to her, do you?" Marcus asked.

"No, won't be a problem. That's kind of you." Eric grabbed his two cups and headed for the door.

James picked up the London Fog and his tea then followed Eric to the antique store. Reaching the front door, he felt like he'd already had three cups of tea. Taking a long breath, he willed his nerves to calm. What was it about this woman that tangled him up inside? He'd been able to keep all women at a distance for years, but not Judy.

"Good morning, you two." Judy floated across the hardwood floor, her face bright with cheer.

"Here. It's a London Fog," James mumbled. "Oh, um, good morning to you both." Dang, he sounded awkward.

Judy's eyes went wide. "How'd you know that was my drink? Well, aren't you just full of surprises."

"Uh—"

"So, come on over here," Judy continued. "I have some books to look through and a few staging pieces out. We'll sit down and try to figure out what you like best."

He wanted to explain he didn't really know her drink and that he didn't buy it, but she'd already moved toward the back of the store, rambling on about how they should stage the farmhouse.

"Oh, I've also made some scones for breakfast. Is blueberry still your favorite?"

"Yes, I—"

"Good. Have a seat here." She took a sip of her drink and hummed. "Perfection. Thank you so much."

"Uh, you're welcome." He shot a quick glance at Eric, who stood next to Lisa leaning against the large, wooden furniture where the register sat. He meant to tell her the truth, but it felt like he'd already lost his chance. Mentioning it now would only make things more awkward. He wasn't a liar, but...heck, he didn't know what he was doing.

"Hey, Mom. I have a meeting this morning. Would you mind giving James a ride back to the house before the contractors arrive?"

"I don't mind, but what about Lisa? I don't want to leave her here alone."

"I'm fine," Lisa said. "I want to work. Let me concentrate on the store while you work on fixing up that house for my wedding."

"You shouldn't over-exert yourself." Judy turned to face James. "I'll call Richard and have him stop in here on the way to the farm. He'll give you a lift."

James scooted the chair out from the table where all the books and merchandise sat. He didn't like the idea of Richard in Judy's store. Not at all. "Well, I'd hoped we could order some pieces for upstairs, too."

Eric pulled Lisa into his side, and she mouthed *thank you*.

"Oh." Judy was silent for a moment. "But I didn't take any measurements. I didn't think—"

"I know. I just want to finish the entire house as much as possible, in honor of Mother."

Judy sat down in the chair next to him, but swiveled to face Eric and Lisa. "You sure you'll be okay here?"

"Yes, I promise. If I even feel a twinge of early labor I'll call Eric and you immediately, okay?"

Judy turned back to James. "Okay, I guess I'm headed to your place after this."

"Great." James leaned over a magazine that Judy had opened and pointed at an image. He tried to concentrate, but found himself focusing more on her floral perfume.

"You like this?" she asked.

"Yes."

"Oh, I think this would be darling in the sitting room." She touched his hand with her soft fingers and his gut flipped. She glanced over at him, her green eyes pools of sparkling seawater he could swim in for eternity.

"James? Earth to James. What about this one?"

He straightened and eyed the yellow thing she referred to as a settee. "Yep, that's nice. Mother would've liked that."

Judy pressed the page down with her palm, spreading the magazine open further. "I know your mother would've liked it. That's why I chose it. But do you?"

James didn't know what to say. "I've never really picked out furniture before. I'm not sure. I mean, I like it. It's warm and looks comfortable. I guess for a sitting room it looks like it would be good to sit on."

Judy laughed aloud. "Yes, I think you're right."

"Now I know why your apartment looks the way it does," Eric chuckled. "Not that mine ever looked better."

Judy looked between them then redirected her attention to her work. "Do you know anything about different styles? I mean, do you like modern, contemporary, classical, Tuscan, craftsman, mid-century modern—"

James shook his head. "I'm not sure I know the difference."

She smiled and fetched a book from another shelf. "This is modern," she said, pointing to a picture. The couch reminded him of his apartment back in Miami. Its white fabric, straight lines and hard cushions looked cold and harsh. "No, I don't like that."

She snapped the book closed and pulled out another book. "What about this?"

"Not as much as what you picked out," he said.

After four more books, he discovered he had traditional taste.

Eric walked by and kissed Judy on the cheek. "Need to go,

Mom. You should be heading out soon, too, if you want to make it back by delivery time."

"Oh, did Richard call?"

"No, but one of his trucks just went by." He smiled. "Have a good day, you two. Try to stay out of trouble."

Judy sprung to life, closing books, shoving a few catalogs into bags. James stood when she did, a courtesy instilled in his brain from his youthful days when his mother pounded manners into him.

She backed away, but he slipped his hand over hers to take the heavy bag. They stood there for a moment, looking at each other.

"I'll take that for you," he finally managed.

She released her hold and turned to Lisa. "Please take care, dear."

They kissed each other's cheeks then Lisa stepped toward him and gave him a peck on both of his cheeks. He could only stand there like a crazy, old man holding bags of books.

"Have a good day," Lisa said.

Tossing everything in the trunk, he hopped into the passenger seat. They listened to the radio while she drove.

Once they turned onto the street leading to the farm Judy turned off her classical music and eyed him. "It's time for my Psych 102 lesson. Why'd you say there was another reason I couldn't forgive Cathy?"

James clutched the door handle. What had gotten into him yesterday? Yes, he believed she still had some jealousy when it came to Cathy and him, but he didn't have to insinuate it. "Nothing. I was just kidding around."

"No, you weren't." Judy turned down the drive, waiting until they were parked before she continued. "You think I still have feelings for you and that jealousy is the reason I can't forgive her." She opened her car door. "I guess you don't need a refund on that fancy degree after all."

Chapter Nineteen

JUDY SCURRIED to greet Richard at his truck. What had possessed her to be so bold? She must have lost her mind.

"Good morning, Richard. Sorry for being late. It looks like your men have already unloaded most of it."

"No worries, sugar. You can make it up to me." Richard winked. The man was exhausting at times, but she'd made it plain to him she wasn't interested when he put the moves on her a few years ago.

"It's my fault," James said, coming up behind her. So, I guess I'll have to make it up to you. Feel free to tack it onto my bill." James' hand rested on the crook of her elbow in almost a possessive way. "I put the bags at the front door. We better get started if you want to order. Didn't you say something about needing to have the order in by this afternoon?"

"You're right. It's already nearing ten. Thanks again, Richard." She halted a few feet away. "Aren't you coming?"

James didn't even look back at her, only remained facing Richard. "I'll settle up with Richard and then be right in."

She grabbed one of the bags, the one with her tape measure and bedroom furniture catalogs before heading up the stairs.

Deciding she should start at the top room—James' old bedroom in the attic—and work her way down, she trudged up the narrow steps to the top. The white wood paneling and pale blue walls hadn't changed in years. She dropped the bag on his old bed and opened the window for fresh air. It slid easy, smelling of WD-40.

The men still stood near the truck, both with a defensive posture. What was going on between those two? Some sort of old school boy debate? But they'd greeted each other like old chums yesterday. She knew they hadn't gotten along well before James left for basic. Heck, some of his parting words had been a warning to stay away from Richard, but that was so long ago.

She retrieved her tape measure and eyed the room. Would he agree to change this to an office? It would make an amazing room to work in. With the white paneling, perhaps a crystal chandelier at the roof point and the right furniture would make an inspiring space. One she, herself would want to work in.

Heavy footsteps warned of James' approach. "You up here?"

"Yes, in your old room," she called down.

He entered with a furrowed brow and tight lips.

"What's going on between you two? Perhaps a little jealousy of your own?" she teased, half hoping he'd respond in a way that indicated she was on to something.

"It's not that."

She sat on the edge of the bed, deflated. "Then what?"

He sighed. "I guess there's been enough secrets kept from you over the years. In honor of us clearing the air, I'll tell you. It's about Cathy."

Cathy. Why was it always about Cathy Mitchell? She rolled the catalog into a tight tube and thought it made a great weapon to swat the pesky woman.

"It's not like that, so put your weapon down and relax." James sat to her side, the bed lowering, tilting her into him, but he didn't move away. In fact, he leaned back into her.

"Long story short, the night before I left for basic that man tried to force himself on Cathy. I'd heard rumors about him, but never thought much about it. As far as I knew, he'd never done anything beyond guilting some poor girls into bed, but according to Cathy he was a little intoxicated that night and upset about something."

Judy gasped then covered her mouth.

"What is it?"

"I might have been the reason. Oh dear, it was so long ago I'd forgotten." Judy worried her hands, the memory of that night coming back to her. "I never said anything because you were leaving and I didn't want to distract you."

James covered her hands with his. "What? Did he do something to you?" An air of hatred she'd never heard from him before seeped into his voice.

"No. Nothing like that." At his raised eyebrow, she added, "I swear. He just professed his feelings for me and I rejected him. The next day he was angry and rude to me, then put the moves on Cathy. I saw them leave together but I didn't say anything to her. She was already upset that I'd taken you from her, I couldn't tell her about Richard, too." She sighed. "I was young and stupid."

James let out a long breath. "Thank goodness."

"Did he...I mean, was she okay? I'd feel awful—"

James kissed the top of her hand, sending an electric pulse up her arm and through her entire body. "She decked him. He never had a chance."

Judy chuckled. "That'a girl. I would've never forgiven myself."

"Kind of like Cathy's never forgiven herself." James squeezed her hand before letting go and standing, taking her breath with him.

His lips had touched her skin, leaving a permanent mark on her heart. Did it mean anything? Was he reconsidering leaving at the end of the two weeks? For the first time in years, dare she hope to find happiness?

"Time to work. We're on a tight schedule and all," James said. He'd been worried about Richard, but he didn't seem to realize that Richard couldn't hurt her. Not the way James' words crushed her under their weight of hopelessness.

Chapter Twenty

WAITING for the crew to arrive the next morning, James wished he had a car. Not that he wanted to leave the house. He felt like a foreigner in his own hometown, with the whispers and gawking looks. But he would've liked to have taken Judy a London Fog. A thank you for all her hard work. She'd insisted he didn't pay her for her hours, that it was her gift to his mother, but he could still show his gratitude.

She deserved the best in life, she always did. While he couldn't give that to her, he could give her a London Fog, even without a car. This *was* the twenty-first century after all. He grabbed his cell from the kitchen table and searched for the coffee shop online. Clicking the phone number on the website, it connected.

"Coffee Bliss, how can I help you?"

"Hi. Is this Marcus?" James asked.

"Yes, sir. Mr. B, right?"

"Just call me James. Can I ask you for a favor? I'd like to order a London Fog for Judy. Actually, I'd like to order one every weekday morning for the rest of this week and next. I'll give you my credit card and I'll pay for a delivery charge."

"No need for the delivery charge. I'd be happy to run it down to her shop. Oh, wait. Actually, she just walked in. You want to talk to her?"

James gripped the railing. "No. Just let me give you my credit card number and that will be it."

"Well, how 'bout you settle up before you leave?"

James meandered down the steps, eyeing the front garden. "You sure?"

"Yeah. We're pretty slammed here right now. Just stop in anytime," Marcus said before the line went dead.

It was a small gesture. Perhaps he could think of something better later. Still, he hoped it would put a smile on her face. God, he loved that smile. If only he could be with her to see it.

The crew arrived early and the work began. All the hammering, sawing, and music drove him to leave his home. With his pounding head, he thought about walking into the town, but it would take him a good while, and he didn't want to be that far away if there was an issue with the house.

Instead, he decided to head to the old suspension bridge. He hadn't seen it since he'd been back. It was probably only a few threads across the river by now.

James found the foreman around back, looking over his notes. "Hey, I'm gonna take a walk. If you need me you've got my cell. I'll just be over at the old bridge, so it shouldn't take long."

"Sure, man. Don't blame you. Looks like something out of a dystopian movie in there. I don't know how I'm going to manage finishing this in three, let alone the two days Richard demanded."

"I know you'll do your best. I'm here if you need an extra set of hands."

"Ha. I need twenty or thirty."

The foreman returned to his notes and James ambled toward the woods behind his house, down the hill and over two more to the river. The gently flowing water gave off a pleasant, trickling sound. The town hadn't had a good rain since he'd arrived. When they did, the river would sound like a wild beast roaring through the valley. To his surprise, the old rope bridge still hung from either side of the ridge. He'd spent many of his youthful days here. Even as a teen, he'd come here when there was something on his mind. An issue he needed to work out for himself.

He stepped on the first board, wondering if it was still sturdy enough to support his weight, unlike the step in his home. Flashes of the blood and terror that ripped through his soul caused him to pause. He hadn't had a nightmare or episode in days. In fact, he'd been more relaxed than he could remember. Perhaps this place wasn't so bad for him after all.

His phone rang and he stepped back from the bridge. Judy's face appeared on the display. Well, a picture of the side of her face that he'd taken at the shop when she wasn't looking. "Hello?"

"Hey, I hear I have you to thank for my beverage this morning."

"Yes, just a little thank you for all your help."

"Is that the only reason?" Judy asked.

James rubbed his chin. "Yes. I mean, I don't know how I'd do this without you. You've been amazing." He paused then said, "I had a question, though."

"What's that?"

James took a long breath. Could he stay here longer? Heck, he had a ton of vacation time. He could stay another month, maybe even two and get the place fixed up right. "The foreman said he doesn't think he can get the work done in two days. We might have to postpone the wedding and—"

"Oh no, we don't. Eric will run off to the courthouse instead, and I'm not letting them skimp on their wedding. This entire town is looking forward to seeing those two get hitched. Why doesn't the foreman think he can get it done?"

James kicked a stray pebble, his shoulders slumped. "I don't know. He said something about not having enough hands."

"I see." The line was silent for a moment then she said, "Okay, well, I'm sure something will work out. Keep me posted. I've got to go to Oakmont this afternoon to handle an estate sale, but I'll check in later. Have a good day."

"You, too." James heard the phone click and he shoved it back in his pants pocket. How stupid was he to think she wanted him to stick around? This project was in the honor of his mother, for Eric and Lisa. It wasn't about them. He'd been so stupid.

Marching back to the house, he threw himself into helping. He'd make sure it all got done. Unfortunately, the day ended then the next, but the work still wasn't complete. On the third day, no one showed. Not even Judy.

Chapter Twenty-One

J AMES BOLTED OUT of bed and grabbed his phone from the dresser. "Hello?"

"Hey, Mr. B. It's Marcus."

James wiped the sleep from his eyes. "Hi, Marcus. What can I do for you?"

"It's probably nothing, but I thought I should call. You know how you asked me to take a beverage to Mrs. G at the antique store each weekday?"

"Yes."

"Well, they're not open. They weren't open yesterday either. Usually they're open six days a week. What do you want me to do?"

James bit at a stray cuticle. "Don't worry about it. Just plan on delivering one on Monday. Judy probably got caught up at the estate sale or something. Thanks for letting me know."

"Sounds good. Talk to you later."

James checked his voicemails and texts, but there were none. Part of him felt relieved that Judy was probably caught up with something and that was why she hadn't called or come by, but in the next breath he worried something had happened. He found Eric in his contacts and hit *call*. It went straight to voicemail.

His hands shook. He sat on the edge of the bed and took three cleansing breaths then clicked Judy's number. Again, straight to voicemail. Something was going on and he needed to know what.

Cathy.

If anyone knew what was going on, she would. He found her number in his contacts and braced himself. Darkness gnawed at him and he fought for control. The anxiety wouldn't win, not until he knew for sure there was a reason to be upset.

"James?"

"Cathy. I'm sorry to bother you, but I can't get a hold of Judy. Eric and Judy's phones go straight to voicemail and I don't have Lisa's number."

"Lisa wouldn't answer anyway."

"What? You know what's going on?" When she didn't answer, James fought the tremble in his voice, but lost. "Please, tell me."

Cathy sighed. "Calm down. Judy's fine. Lisa went into labor on Thursday night. She's been in the hospital ever since. Eric and Judy haven't left her side and their phones probably don't work in the hospital."

James heard a car door slam and raced to the window. The nursery trucks were there with all the plants. "Thanks, Cathy. I've got to go." He hit *end* and threw on his clothes before racing downstairs.

Some shaggy haired kid waved him over. "Hey, Mr. Benjamin. I've got some trees here for you."

James shuffled to the front of the truck. "Great, thanks so much. Hey, would you mind giving me a ride to the hospital. It's important."

"Sure, man. No worries. Hey, Jake. Give Mr. Benjamin a ride to the hospital, would ya?"

Another young man placed a potted plant on the ground then straightened. "Sure, just need to unload the rest."

James grabbed two pots at a time and helped the boy unload the truck. "Okay, let's go."

The young man pulled a cloth from his back pocket and wiped his brow. "Hop in."

As they putted down the drive, James wanted to reach over and press the gas pedal down. For a kid, he drove like an old-fart.

"I heard you returned from the dead. That's cool. Name's Joe, by the way."

"Thanks for the ride, Joe." James kept his gaze fixed out the window. Lowering his hand from his mouth, he noticed the spot of blood where his cuticle once was. Darn bad habit.

Joe continued to pepper him with questions, which James did his best to dodge, until they reached the hospital parking lot.

James opened the door and hopped out before the truck had stopped completely. "Thanks for the ride, Joe."

"Sure, man. Good luck with that lost love thing." Joe saluted then took off.

James just stood there a moment, staring after him. *It doesn't matter*, he told himself. He already knew how the kid had found out his life story. Small town living hadn't changed, and probably never would.

Rushing through the automatic doors, he searched for the information desk.

"Can I help you, sir?" asked a woman behind a long counter.

"Yes, I'm looking for a patient's room. She went into preterm labor on Thursday."

"I'd be happy to ring her room. What's the last name?"

James thought for a moment, but couldn't recall. "Her fiancé is Eric Gaylord and her soon-to-be mother-in-law is Judy Gaylord.

"I'm sorry, sir, but I won't be able to look it up that way," the receptionist said.

James shoved his hands in his pockets. "Right. I should have thought of that." *Now what?*

"James? What are you doing here?"

He pivoted on his heels and saw Judy a few feet away. "I just heard about Lisa. Is she okay?"

She smoothed her wrinkled clothes and squinted through her swollen eyes. "She's fine. We're taking her home later. But what do you mean just? Jimmy was supposed to tell you yesterday."

"Jimmy?"

"The foreman."

James shook his head. "He wasn't there. Richard stopped by and said he was down sick."

"Oh, I'm so sorry. I was going to call, but my phone didn't work inside, and I didn't want to leave Eric. He's been beside himself with worry."

James ran his fingers through his short hair. "It's okay. I just thought something might be wrong, that you might have been in an accident or something."

Judy came closer, so close she nearly touched him. "You were worried about me?"

"Not worried...but concerned I hadn't heard from you."

Judy smiled and lifted his right hand. "I'd say your missing cuticle tells a different story. Guess you never broke that habit, huh?"

He chuckled. "No. Lord knows I've tried."

"Well, Lisa's sleeping, but I need to get my place ready for her. She's going to be staying there for a few nights while she's still on bed rest. Wait," she glanced around, "how did you get here?"

James shoved his hands in his pockets. "I hitched a ride from Joe."

"Joe?" Judy asked.

"Yes, the plant guy."

Judy laughed. "If you don't mind stopping at my place, I'll give you a ride back after that."

"That would be great." James followed her to her car. "I guess the wedding won't be happening now. Not like you'd planned."

"Bite your tongue, James Benjamin. It is and it will."

"But I thought she was on bed rest."

"For a few days, but she'll be able to stand up at her wedding. Now, where are we on all that?"

"I'm afraid the construction isn't done. I can't finish it all myself and Bellings didn't show today."

Judy pressed her lips together. "Well, we'll just have to work extra hard starting tomorrow."

It was a short drive to her home, a craftsman style with big potted plants out front.

"Come on in and have a seat." Judy waved at a couch near a large stone fireplace. She sat at his side and placed her feet on the coffee table. "I guess we'll need a few more people to help us, but we'll pull it off." She yawned then leaned her head back.

"I'll do whatever I can, but he said there are no more men to hire."

"Oh, hogwash. We'll figure it out." She closed her eyes and began to breathe slow and heavy.

He curled her into his side and held her while she slept. His tension faded and he pressed a kiss to the top of her head. "Sweet dreams, darling."

Chapter Twenty-Two

JUDY STEPPED out of the house onto the front porch, noticing the vast amount of work that still needed to be done prior to the wedding. Paint the stairs and molding, repair the front door, clean the windows. Spotting James stretched out on the swing, dressed in a flannel top, work pants, and boots, she smiled. "Made you sustenance before we start this crazy day. It was a challenge in the kitchen, too. Good thing I brought the ingredients or you would've had some mystery cereal."

He rose to his feet. Always the perfect gentleman. "I never did make it to the store. I heard your phone. Was it Eric? How's Lisa?"

"Good. Much better. Eric said the doctor gave approval for the wedding as long as she rests until then."

James took a plate and smiled. "Yum. Scones. You're spoiling me."

"I think you deserve some spoiling." Judy handed him his hot tea and settled in the swing, him sitting down beside her. "Sorry about falling asleep on you last night."

James held the plate to his nose and sniffed. "I didn't mind. Actually, I have a confession to make. I enjoyed holding you."

"Really?"

James nodded and took a bite of his breakfast, Judy smiling at how his eyes rolled back in his head as he savored the taste. "Mother always said you were gifted in the kitchen. These are delicious."

"Thanks." Judy sipped her tea. "I guess I have a confession to make, too. I enjoyed you holding me."

They both rocked in silence for a few moments while they finished their scones. Judy longed to ask him to stay, but was it her right? Didn't he need to return to Miami?

"I fell asleep, too." James looked out over the front lawn with a far off gaze. "Shouldn't have done that."

She touched his forearm. "Why?"

"I've never allowed myself to fall asleep with anyone in the same house with me since the night I almost killed my mother."

"Never? What about when your mom moved to Miami? Didn't she live with you? You said she moved there to be with you."

He shook his head, still absently staring at nothing. "No. I've never even fallen asleep at my desk. I don't usually sleep a lot, but for some reason when you snuggled up next to me, I drifted off."

"Good, now you know it's safe." Judy ran her nails up and down his arm. "You don't have to be scared to touch people, or sleep next to them. You're not that person anymore."

James sighed. "I don't know. Maybe. It's just too big a risk."

Judy touched his chin, guiding his head around to look at her. "One I'm willing to take."

He smiled, one of his dashing *I'm-James-Benjamin* smiles. "The way you look at me, I almost believe anything's possible." Taking the last bite of his scone, he wiped his hands on his pants. "What do you think about visiting me in Miami?"

"I've never been to Miami. It could be fun." She hesitated. Dare she say it? "Of course, you could always stay here."

James traced circles around her palm. "Isn't this our past? If I ever did trust myself in the same room with you, don't you want to look to the future? Live in a new place, make new memories instead of facing old, haunting ones?"

Judy couldn't think with his fingers gently sweeping across her hand. She closed her fingers around his. "This place might be our past and present, but it's also my future. My grandbaby is about to be born. My son is here...my business. I can't leave."

James pulled his hand free and leaned back in the swing. "I understand."

"You could give it a chance here," she urged, trying to keep the begging tone from her voice. "Stay a little longer, just to see how things go."

James huffed. "I'm an outsider now. The freak who said he was dead and now returns. Why would the town ever welcome me back?"

"That's crazy talk. Now, you listen to me, James Benjamin. This town has always loved you. You were the star athlete, the hero gone to war, the boy every girl swooned for in high school." She nudged him. "Besides, we've got a lot of crazies around here that could use your help."

James laughed. "We don't like to call our clients crazy."

"Sorry, but in this town we've just got plain crazy." She stood and listened to the distant hum of approaching vehicles. "Sometimes crazy can be good."

His hand rested on her shoulder as he came to stand beside her. "I wish I could try, for you. Don't you deserve better, though? A whole man, one you don't have to lock yourself in a separate room at night for?"

She twirled to face him and found herself in his arms. Inhaling his flannel, leather, and spicy aroma, she felt off-kilter for a moment and placed her hands on his hips to remain standing. "Can I ask you something?"

"Sure. Anything."

His gaze moved to her lips, and she nearly lost the words before she could speak again. "If you were one of your patients, and you saw he had an amazing woman, a town that loved him, and a possible future, what would you tell him?"

"I don't know. Amazing women are hard to find." He brushed his thumb across her lips "I only found one in my lifetime." He lowered his hand and stepped away, pacing the porch. "As for the town, I'm still an outsider. I haven't been around long enough to earn back anyone's trust. I lied to everyone. Why would they welcome me back?"

"Again, I think you better get a refund on that fancy degree of yours."

The vehicles rumbled closer. She glanced back at the front lawn and the sight of the first truck breaking the tree line then smiled and marched straight to him. "Does that look like a town that doesn't love you?"

Chapter Twenty-Three

JAMES PRESSED his palms against the railing, supporting his body as he watched truck after car after SUV come down his driveway. They all parked on his front lawn. If it wasn't for the updated vehicles, he'd swear he'd stepped back into one of his mother's big picnic events, or town chili cook-offs she used to host.

"Marcus? Cathy? Even the waitress from the café?"

"Yep. When the town found out about our issue, they all decided to chip in. There's others, too. They'll be rotating in and out during the day due to work shifts and stuff."

"There must be thirty cars," James mumbled, still unable to process what he was seeing. "You really do have special powers. I told you that once, remember?"

Judy took his elbow and guided him down the front porch steps. "Yes. You told me one person couldn't do everything I did, so you needed to come sneak into my window to see if I remained human after dark. Of course, it was just a ploy to get into my bed."

"And I thought I was being smooth."

"Oh, you were smooth all right. I just had my powers to deflect your charm."

James patted her hand and laughed.

Marcus approached, a teenaged girl beside him. "Hi, Mr. B. This is my girlfriend, Rose."

"Nice to meet you, Rose."

The girl shook his hand, but her eyes were absorbing the home behind him. "Nice to meet you, too. Marcus had nice things to say about you. I've always loved this house."

"We all have. The mayor said he believes it's a historical landmark that needs to be preserved. Asked some of the townspeople to donate time and supplies, with it being an election year and all." Cathy winked and nodded. "We'll have this place ready. Don't you worry." She stepped around them, avoiding Judy who released his arm to greet some folks he didn't recognize.

"Where do you want us to start?" Marcus asked.

James shrugged. "I'm not the boss here. I think you better check with Judy."

"Yes, sir. Consider it done, Mr. B." Marcus saluted him before heading to Judy.

James offered Cathy his arm and guided her to the steps. "Cathy. I spoke to Judy."

She jerked away and busied herself with the bag slung over her shoulder. "You shouldn't have done that."

He looked between them. "She misses you. I can tell."

"I'm here to help save a wedding and the sale of this old house. Now that the Mayor's on board, you won't have to worry about them tearing it down. If you're still serious about wanting to give it away, here's your chance. The town is thinking about taking it on as a tourist site."

"The farm? Why?"

Cathy shrugged. "Someone might have made the Mayor believe there was some significant historical facts about this land dating back to the Civil War."

"What gave him that idea?"

Cathy shrugged again. "Don't know. You don't look so happy,

though. Isn't that what you wanted, a way to retreat out of town quickly?"

"Yes, of course. Although, I'll wait until after the wedding and see if there are any prospective buyers before dumping the property. That wouldn't be a smart business decision."

"So, you'll hang onto it until after the wedding because it's good business? You sure that's the only reason?"

"I don't know what you mean," James mumbled.

"That's right. You don't have your *sights* on any other reason." Cathy shook her head. "Best go clean those windows. They ain't gonna clean themselves."

Judy waved, and he realized the entire time he'd been talking to Cathy he'd been watching Judy's every move.

Person after person approached and either introduced themselves or wanted to visit about the old days. It took a good thirty minutes before he'd met everyone, and another thirty until Judy and he had everyone assigned to a task.

All the townsfolk were nice, giving, and loving. He'd forgotten what it felt like to have a home with community and family. It was...nice.

Rounding the back of the house, Judy lifted a paintbrush and handed it to him. "Get to work." Then she turned to Marcus and Rose. "Hey, you two, there are snacks out front."

"Okay, Mrs. B. I mean, Mrs. G." Marcus blushed then hurried around the side of the house, leaving them alone.

James dipped his paintbrush into the white liquid on the table and began to paint the wood that Marcus and his girlfriend had finished cleaning. "Bossy now, are we?"

"Someone needs to move you in a direction. You don't seem to know what you want."

"I know what I want," James quipped.

Judy placed her hand on her hip in that *don't-lie-to-me* smug expression she'd perfected. "James Benjamin, you know you don't have a clue. But if you did, then it seems you're too scared to go for what you want."

"I'm not scared. If I want something, I'll make it happen."

"Sure, whatever you say."

Dang, that woman was exasperating, conniving, and a handful. And he wanted her. He tossed his paintbrush down and tugged her to him. "You sure you're not the one who's scared? You're trembling." Before she had a chance to respond, he claimed her lips with the passion of a seventeen-year-old boy about to leave for war.

Chapter Twenty-Four

JUDY AMBLED out onto the front porch, rubbing her shoulders. With a list in her hand, she sat on the swing and double-checked her schedule. Tomorrow and the next day, she had help from eight am to eight pm. At that point, she hoped to be able to start moving furniture in and hanging curtains.

She rested the pencil's eraser against her lips and smiled. That kiss had pushed her through the day, and probably the rest of her life. It had been years since she had a bone deep, knee wobbling, oh-my-God kind of kiss.

"Hey, I've got a peace offering. A cup of tea to soothe your weary bones." Cathy stood a few feet away, her eyes pleading.

Judy didn't know if it was still the kiss-high she was on, or if she just didn't have the energy to hate anyone anymore, but for the first time in days she wanted her old best friend back. "Sure. Have a seat."

Cathy sat by her side and handed her the cup of tea. "You know, I've seen a change in him. You're good for him. He's good for you, too."

Judy caught a bit of flannel shirt scoot by the window. James had put Cathy up to this, but no matter, she was here and it was past time for them to talk.

"You know, he's really hoping we work things out," Judy said. "He's tried to convince me it was all his fault. That man has carried the weight of his lie for so many years. I guess I can see how it must've been tough for you to keep that secret. I'm not going to pretend that I completely understand that choice, or that I'm not still holding a grudge, but I'll admit I could've handled it better."

Cathy snickered. "I thought you handled it better than expected. I was sure my house would be burnt down, my car keyed, or I'd wake up to find a dark figure wielding a butcher knife."

Judy chuckled. "Please. Not my style. I prefer a quiet murder with no evidence or witnesses. Poison perhaps."

Cathy glanced at the cup of tea in her hand then rested it back on her knee. "You know, for what it's worth, that secret has torn me up since I made the promise to keep it. I almost told you, too."

Judy quirked her head to the side. "When?"

"After Eric was born, when I was told James would be released from the hospital."

"What changed your mind?"

Cathy shrugged. "I went to your house, but when I looked through the window you and Michael were sitting on the couch together holding Eric. You looked happy for the first time in forever. Then I thought I'd wait and see how James did once he was released."

"And what happened then?"

"He disappeared. His mother wouldn't tell me where he went. Eventually, she asked me for photos of you guys. I didn't know at first that she sent them to James. He's followed your life all this time. The man never stopped loving you."

Judy bowed her head, shame filling her. "If I had—"

"Don't do that, Judy. The entire thing was a mess. If you want to blame someone, blame those Godforsaken Vietcongs or the bureaucrats that put him there. You've both beat yourselves up enough."

Judy sighed. "You're right. All this guilt has eaten all of us up for so many years, perhaps we need to let it go. What you did...I don't agree with, but I respect that you did it for the right reasons. I don't know if we'll ever be close again, but I'm willing to try to mend the fence. At the very least, behave like a civilized woman in public."

Cathy smiled. "I'd like that." She stood, sending the swing rocking. "So, was it as good as it was back in 1970?"

"What?"

"His kiss."

Judy felt heat surge to her cheeks. "What...How...Were you spying on us?"

"No. I didn't have to. You were doing the same thing you did back in high school when you two would disappear behind the building at lunch. You were touching your lips with that goofy grin. It was a tell-tale sign then and it's sure as heck a tell-tale sign now." Cathy winked then headed into the house just as James stepped onto the porch. "Way to go, boy."

James' brow creased. "What was that about?"

"Apparently I'm an open book." Judy laughed.

James sat next to her on the swing. "Great, I wanted you two to be civil again. But that secret language you two have between you, I never did understand it."

"Don't worry. We won't be braiding each other's hair anytime soon."

James lifted his arm around her shoulders and leaned her into him. "I can't believe how much work we accomplished today. I'm exhausted."

"Me, too." Judy stuck her papers into her folder. "It would

probably be better if I just stayed the night here. I can sleep in your parents'—"

James stiffened beside her. "No."

She sat forward and turned to him, taking his hand in hers. "James, if you want, I'll lock the bedroom door. We can do this. You don't have to be scared anymore."

"Falling asleep by your side for an hour on the couch is one thing. You being in the house with me all night is another. I won't risk your safety. I-I care about you too much." His voice choked and he stood, walking over to lean against the railing. "If I have night terrors, I'll hurt you. I can't help myself."

Judy went to his side, rubbing small circles on his back as she tried to soothe him. "It's okay. I won't push. I'll go home."

"Thank you," he whispered.

"Cathy's the last one inside. I'll walk out with her." She turned toward the front door. "You rest and I'll see you tomorrow."

James slid his hand over the railing and covered Judy's. "I— There's something I want to say."

"Yes?" She held her breath, hoping he'd changed his mind. For him to let go and accept that he could have her in his life.

"I...um...well, thank you." His jaw tensed and his distant gaze looked like pools of darkness.

Unable to face the pain in his eyes a moment longer, Judy leaned her head against his shoulder. "You already said that."

"Right." James straightened. "Well, I'll walk you ladies out. I don't want you driving too late. Will I see you tomorrow?"

"Absolutely."

James escorted them to their cars then went back inside the empty house, his shoulders slumped. The man looked like he'd just been beaten like a bad dog.

Why had she pushed him? It was too much for him, too soon, but the clock was ticking down the days and she didn't want him to leave. Was Cathy right? Was she selfish? Did she want more than he could give? All she knew was that look on his face broke her heart.

Cathy stuffed her bucket and supplies in the trunk and rounded the car. "What happened? You two were so happy earlier."

Judy sighed. "I pushed too hard. You were right."

"About what?"

Judy grabbed the handle of her door. "I am selfish. I need to let him go."

Chapter Twenty-Five

JAMES WAITED on the front porch, grasping the picnic basket in his hands, his belly flopping around like a catfish on dry land. Judy had him all tied up in knots like she always had. Just the idea of seeing her smiling face made his day brighter.

He set the basket down and paced. The night was cool, which made it even better for snuggling out by the river. She'd been busy helping with the final touches on the inside painting, and he'd barely had five minutes alone with her. Another day of refurbishment and decorating and the house was starting to come together. Now that the crew was packing up and heading out, he longed to steal another kiss, or hold her hand while they walked.

Tonight he'd tell her he never stopped loving her, that he wanted to try to figure things out. He wanted to stay in Sweetwater County after the wedding so they could have more time together. If they took it slow...maybe they could try another nap on the couch with her son at home. Or if they fell asleep at the river this evening... Marcus would be at the picnic. If they cuddled up on the blanket and dozed... He was a big kid. He'd be able to protect Judy from James. The thought of holding her under the stars made him feel alive again.

If only he had some guarantee he wouldn't harm her. Maybe she was right. It was time for him to try. If he was talking to one of his patients he'd think they were insane for worrying about this after not having a night terror for so long, but it still plagued him.

Marcus thumped across the porch. "Hey, Mr. B. Let me take that for you."

"I brought some potato salad, too. I hope that's okay," Rose said.

"I love potato salad. Thanks. I guess I better go tell Judy about our picnic."

"She doesn't know?" Marcus asked.

"No. It's a surprise. Cathy helped plan it. I'll go tell her." James shuffled into the room and found Richard holding a stepladder for Judy while she hung some material over the window.

"How does that look?" Judy asked, still facing the wall.

Richard kept his gaze on her backside. "Looks great."

"Judy, can I speak to you?" James heard the anger in his voice and cleared his throat.

Judy shook her head. "I'm busy right now."

Cathy entered from the kitchen. "Why don't I hold that up for you and you and James can see what you think from back there."

"Sure, thanks."

Richard helped her down the ladder and James had to suppress the urge to break his hand.

While Judy eyed the material from the back of the room, James leaned in to whisper in her ear, not wanting Richard to overhear him. "Marcus, Rose, and I are taking you on a twilight picnic. I thought we could look at the stars."

Judy pushed back her shoulders. "Nope, I'm going to have to go back and order a different material. Those colors are just all wrong." She sauntered away without a word and folded the cloth. "I'll head back now and get the new order placed so I'll have it in time for the house showing."

"House showing?" James asked.

"Yes, I found some people who want to come by and look at it. They stopped in the store yesterday evening and asked about homes in the area. They'll be here Friday."

"Oh." James tried to keep the disappointment from his voice. "Well, they can see it without curtains. You don't need to do that now. You've worked so hard today already."

"I need to get back before dark anyway. I want to check on Lisa before I head home. Looks like most of the crew is gone, so if you guys don't mind, I'll go head out." Judy didn't wait for a response. She just shoved the material in her rolling tote thingy and took off.

He was left standing there, listening to those wheels bump down the front steps.

"You okay?" Cathy asked.

Richard folded the ladder, whistling like a bomb had dropped. Dang, that man rubbed him the wrong way. "See you two tomorrow."

Cathy picked up her supplies. "You need to tell her how you feel. You're not getting any younger."

"I tried, but I didn't want to make her think this would work if it wouldn't. I don't want to hurt her again."

Cathy let out a loud breath. "I know it's none of my business, and you probably don't want to hear it, but it seems to me that every time you try to protect her, you end up hurting her."

All night he tossed and turned, thinking about what Cathy said. She was right. When Judy returned in the morning, he'd tell her how he felt and ask her if she wanted him to stay.

But when morning finally arrived, all the townspeople came, the crew came, and rain came. The only thing that didn't was Judy.

Chapter Twenty-Six

JUDY UNLOCKED the front door of the shop, sat down at the table and picked up her cell. Finding Cathy in her contacts, she texted:

Not going to make it there today. I'm working on orders and need to open shop. Good luck.

Lisa stood up from the chair on the other side of the table.

"Where do you think you're going?" Judy chastised. "I promised Eric you weren't going to move."

"Um, hello? Pregnant lady here drinking a tumbler of water."

Judy smirked. "Okay. Straight to the bathroom then back to your seat until Eric comes to get you for lunch."

Lisa huffed. "I love you, so don't take this the wrong way, but please leave me here and go to the farm. Eric said it was fine."

"No way. I'm not letting you out of my sight."

Lisa sighed then headed to the bathroom. "You mean you want to use me as an excuse."

Judy's phone beeped before she could reply and she spied Cathy's face smiling back at her. She glanced at the text that simply said, *Coward.*

Fumbling through catalogs, she forced her thoughts from

James. She couldn't put him through anymore by demanding he stay, but at the same time she couldn't kiss him, hold him then let him go. She'd fallen for him once and lost him. Her heart couldn't handle that again.

Lisa returned to her seat. "Listen, you made me see the light not too long ago. Now, it's my turn."

Judy held up one hand. "It's not the same thing."

"Don't give me the Judy hand block."

She laughed. "The what?"

"Judy hand block. You do that to dismiss people. Well, I'm not going to let you dismiss me. Now, listen up. You love him and don't you deny it. I see it in your face. You always have and you always will."

"It doesn't matter. We can't be together. He's going back to Miami soon, and honestly, I don't have the strength to let him go."

"Then don't."

"I don't want to talk about this anymore. Please." Judy's voice rose louder than she intended. "I'm sorry," she sighed.

Lisa smiled. "It's okay."

"I don't think Eric would feel that way." She shook her head. "Me raising my voice at a pregnant lady."

"I'm made tougher than that." Lisa folded her hands in front of her. "I wish I could help you the way you helped me, that's all."

"I know, dear." She glanced down at the catalogs then said, "Listen, you can help me. Tomorrow night Eric is going out with the guys, right? Can you ask him to take James with him? I need to oversee some deliveries and installations at his house, but I don't want to see him."

"Eric already planned on inviting him. He's going to pick him up around three in the afternoon, so they can do their final tux fitting and then go to dinner before some bachelor thing." Lisa rolled her eyes.

"Oh my word," Judy gasped. "I didn't plan a bachelorette party for you."

"Please, I beg you, don't!" Lisa smacked her hands to her face. "The last thing I want is to go to a party right now."

"I understand. I just hate to let you down." Judy shook her head.

"You could never let me down. You're not just like a mother to me. You're the only mother I've ever known."

As Lisa's eyes filled with tears, Judy stood up and came around the table. "Oh, darling." She gathered Lisa into a hug. "You're my only daughter, so we're perfect for each other. You know I love you as my own blood."

"I know. It's just these hormones. I keep waiting for something to happen that'll stop the wedding. I want to just go to the courthouse tonight and have the ceremony."

"Don't you worry. Everything's going to be fine. These things always work out."

Lisa leaned back, but kept hold of her hands. "Do they?"

Judy squeezed her fingers. "What do you mean?"

"You and James wanted to wait until he returned, but look what happened. What if something happens with Eric, or—"

"Now, you stop that. Everything's fine. As for James and I, we made choices. We can blame life and how unfair it was, but in the end, we chose what we had, and even now we choose. I could go to that farmhouse right now and tell him how I feel, but I choose not to."

"But why?"

"Because I love him. If you saw the terror in his eyes every time I mention him staying in Sweetwater, you wouldn't ask me that."

Lisa released her hands and sat back down. "I can understand that. If Eric even showed an ounce of fear about marrying me, I'd leave. I love him too much to see him unhappy."

"Well, aren't we a pair. I think I'll make us some tea." Judy went to the kitchen and put the kettle on.

Standing in silence, she thought about all the choices she'd made. If James wanted to stay, he had that choice. If he wanted to be afraid of hurting her, he had the choice to return to Miami. She gripped the side of the counter and fought back the tears.

But can I choose to let him go?

Chapter Twenty-Seven

JAMES HOPPED into Eric's car. "Hey, kid. How are you today? Nervous? Tomorrow's the big day."

"Not at all. I'm ready. I've been ready. Lisa's the most amazing, loving, and caring woman I've ever known."

"I'm happy for you."

Eric turned onto the main road heading into town. "The place looked great."

"That's all your mother's doing." James forced his voice to sound light, conversational. "Um, how is she? I haven't seen her in a couple days."

Eric shrugged. "I haven't seen much of her either. Lisa said she's holding up."

"Holding up? Is everything okay?" A searing fear raced through him.

"She's fine." Eric smiled. "For a man who doesn't want to stay, I think you sound awfully interested."

James unclenched his fists. "I thought about staying. I'd planned a picnic to tell her how I wanted to extend my time here and get to know each other again, but she left in a hurry and I haven't seen her since."

Eric pulled into the parking lot of a strip mall on the edge of town and parked the car. "Listen, do you care about my mother?"

James swallowed a lump in his throat and wiped his sweaty palms down his pant legs. "I love her. I always have and I always will. There's no denying it, but...it's complicated."

"Are you talking about what happened with your mother? Because I think you're hiding behind that. I'm her son and if I trust my mother when she tells me that you'd never hurt her, I believe it. I think you're scared of something else. Losing her again, maybe? Not trusting that things will work out? I'm not a shrink, but I think you need to look at why you really keep pushing her away." Eric opened the door and James followed, splashing through the puddles to a storefront with fancy dresses and tuxedos.

"You and your mother are so much alike. Makes me wonder why I went to school all those years. You two seem to be experts without being educated on the subject." He laughed, trying to mask his realization that Eric was right. He'd been so clouded by emotions that he never considered the rationality behind his issues. "Good thing the rain stopped, I was worried the roads to the farm were going to flood. I just hope it dries out by tomorrow."

Eric opened the door, holding it for James as a bell jingled overhead. "You like changing the subject, don't you, old man?"

Relief came with the sight of the salesman approaching them. "Mr. Gaylord, we have your tuxedo all ready for you. Please follow me."

Eric held up a finger. "Just a second please." He turned back to James. "James, how much time are you going to waste?"

James quirked an eyebrow. "What do you mean?"

"You and my mother have been in love your entire lives. There's a wedding tomorrow, one between two people who've only known each other a few months. How many years are you going to let pass before you discover you missed your chance. You only get so much time in life, you know."

While Eric disappeared into a changing room, James stood at the front of the store, looking out the window, watching people pass by. Life had continued in this town while he was away, yet they still had a place for him. Two women waved at him and he returned the gesture. These were good people. They'd been good to his mother and father. She had raved about how they helped her through the dark times, calling them her 'town family.'

His chest tightened as he looked to the sky. If only he had listened to her when she had begged him to return. "I see it now, Mother," he muttered. "You were right. It's safe here."

The thought of boarding the plane on Sunday made him more anxious than the thought of remaining in Sweetwater County for the rest of his days. More than taking a chance with Judy by his side all night.

I'm safe here. I want to stay, to have a home. To love and be loved.

"You need something, sir?" the salesman said behind him.

He turned around as Eric came out in his penguin suit. "What was that, old man?"

James took a deep breath. "I guess you're the man of the house now, kid. It's on you." He took a step forward. "Will you allow me to ask for your mother's hand in marriage?"

Eric tugged the sleeves of his shirt down to line up with the cuffs of his tail coat. "I'll do one better. You get my mother to say yes, and you're going to share our day tomorrow."

"I couldn't. Tomorrow is for you and Lisa."

Eric chuckled. "Who's idea do you think it was? Lisa's been silently hoping and praying to share our wedding with Mom. You'll make her day the most special one of her life if my mother walks down the aisle with her. Besides, the whole town deserves to see your happy ending. They've all been rooting for you since you arrived. Well, except for Richard Bellings."

James didn't let his unease with the man stir him up inside. This wasn't about Richard, or anyone else in the town.

He spun around to face the sales clerk, his body feeling young and light, peace pouring over him. "I need a tuxedo, by tomorrow." Then he looked at Eric. "Don't say a word to Judy. I'm afraid I hurt her feelings last time she was at the farm. She's been avoiding me since and won't take my calls, but she'll be there tomorrow morning. I need some help though if I'm going to pull this off." He tugged his phone from his pants pocket and hit Cathy's name in his contacts list.

The phone rang through twice before Cathy answered. "Well, you sure did blow it, didn't you?" Cathy said in lieu of a greeting.

"What do you mean?"

She chuckled. "Judy hasn't been out to the farm in days. You listen here, James Benjamin. You're ruining a good thing. She's the best thing that ever happened to you and you're a fool to let her go. Get over yourself. Stop being such a scared little boy and tell her how you feel."

"Cathy—"

"Don't interrupt me. You need to hear this."

"I'm going to ask her to marry me."

Silence.

James laughed aloud. "Well, that's a first. Listening to me now? I need your help. I'm not only asking her to marry me, but Eric and Lisa want a double wedding."

"What?" Cathy stammered. "But how will you get a license and all that by tomorrow?"

James couldn't stop smiling. "The license we can deal with later. I just want to hear her say yes. We have to pull this off by tomorrow evening. I need you to handle any of the girly stuff. Go buy her a dress, or raid her closet or something, flowers, have someone there to do hair, makeup and whatever else girls need for a wedding. I'll take care of the tux and getting the bride to say yes."

"You don't worry about the girly stuff," Cathy assured him. "She's already done all that for being the maid of honor anyway. As for the dress, I've already taken care of that. I'd been hoping this would happen. Don't worry. I've planned accordingly on my end, but you're facing a battle. Good luck convincing her to say yes."

"Thank you, Cathy. Judy might not remember, but I know you were and will always be her best friend." James hit *end* on the phone and turned to Eric. "It's time for us to make some magic, kid. Now, I just have to convince that stubborn mother of yours that she wants to spend the rest of her life with me."

Chapter Twenty-Eight

THE WHITE TENT rose in the backyard, lifting Judy's mood to a new height. Today wasn't about her. It was for Eric and Lisa. She'd be happier for them than she'd be for herself if it was her day.

Samantha, the banquet rental lady, lowered her clipboard. "Thank goodness the rain stopped when it did, Ms. Gaylord. I was worried about the ground being too wet for an outdoor reception."

"It's beautiful. I know this will be a wedding this town will remember for years to come." Perhaps James could sell this to the county as a wedding venue. When she saw him today, she'd mention it to him.

This was it. After today her life would be back to normal again. She'd return to morning tea at the coffee shop, days working at the antique store, and weekends touring estate and garage sales.

Young men paraded in with the eight rectangular tables and a slew of chairs.

"Stagger them so they're not in straight lines," Samantha directed the men. "Linens are in that box."

"It looks like you have everything under control out here. I better go check on the bride and the flowers inside." Judy headed up the back steps, through the kitchen, and up the stairs to the master bedroom.

Lisa sat on the bed, a smile permanently plastered on her face. Warmth flooded her at the sight of her daughter-in-law. She was about to gain an instant family and she hoped it wouldn't stop there. "How are you doing? Keeping your feet up until the ceremony, right?"

"Yes, I'm not doing anything to jeopardize today."

The crunch of gravel drew their attention to the front of the house. Eric and Cathy's cars pulled to a stop and two teens took over to park the cars in the outer pasture.

As she watched, James walked around the vehicles dressed in a black tuxedo. He looked up at the bedroom window, his silver eyes shining so bright it melted her resolve.

Dear Lord. How am I going to stand by that man all day and not fall apart with grief knowing he's leaving me again?

She took a deep breath to calm her emotions and looked back out the window as Cathy handed James a dress bag and directed him inside. She and Eric followed with more bags and all the supplies a bride needed on her big day.

"Hey, Judy," Cathy's voice boomed up the stairs. "Come down here and give us a hand. Stop slacking up there."

Judy turned to Lisa. "You don't move. The groom can't see you before the ceremony."

"You don't buy that old superstition, Judy Gaylord."

"Nope, but it's a good excuse to make sure you stay off your feet."

Judy sauntered down the stairs, keeping her eyes everywhere but on the strong man with broad shoulders and a handsome face. It didn't work.

James met her at the bottom step, took her hand and breath, "You look beautiful."

She tried to slip her hand away, but he gripped it a little tighter. "That's what you're supposed to say to the bride."

James smiled a big teeth-bearing grin that would melt any woman into goo.

"What?"

James tugged her toward the front door. "I'd like to talk to you on the front porch for a minute." It wasn't really a question, but more of a demand as he guided her through the front door.

"I've got so much to do. There isn't any time right now," Judy protested.

"Make time. I've been trying to tell you something for days, but you won't take my calls. You are one stubborn woman, but for once you're going to stand there and listen to what I have to say. Got it?"

Judy narrowed her gaze. "Fine. What's so important?"

James moved a hand to her shoulder. "Do you remember the other day when we were out here and I tried to tell you something? I wanted to tell you how I felt, but I couldn't get the words out."

"I know how you feel and I respect it. The look of terror on your face spoke volumes. You can't have me in your life, I know that." She glanced away. "Please, James, I understand and I don't want to be selfish. I only want what's best for you."

"If you'd stop talking and listen you'd know that you're what's best for me. I love you."

Judy sucked in a quick breath. "What?"

"That's what I've wanted to tell you for days now. I love you. I always have and I always will."

Tears filled Judy's eyes, but she swiped them away. "I love you, too. That's why you have to go."

"You're still not listening to me. I love you and I don't want to go. Ever."

Judy's hands shook and he took them in his, kissing her knuckles.

"I don't know if I can see you every day and not be with you," she choked out. "I'll try, but you ask too much." Tears streaked down her face.

"Oh, Judy." His thumb brushed the tears from her cheek. "I want to be with you while I'm here, always. Day and *night*."

"But...you don't want to sleep next to me. How can we—"

James bent down on one knee in front of her and the air shot from her lungs. Only his grip and the railing behind her kept her standing.

"What are you doing?"

He pulled a box from his pocket and opened it. Martha's sapphire earrings sat on a white satin cushion. "I didn't have time to get a ring yet, but I thought this could cover the something blue. We'll go shopping soon." He cleared his throat. "Judy Gaylord, will you be my wife? To have and to hold, day *and night* for all the days I have left on this planet?"

"I don't understand. You...I—"

James clutched her hands tighter, his gaze pleading. "It took me a while, and a little convincing from your son, but it wasn't about hurting you during the night. Not anymore. It was about losing you again. I realized if all I get is one day on this planet with you, it will be the best day of my life."

Judy's head swam and the tears flowed down her cheeks.

"What's your answer? Will you make me the happiest and most blessed man in the entire world?"

Judy didn't know what to think or do. All these years, and now? They'd wasted so much time, and she wanted him in her life more than air in her lungs.

"Don't leave the man hanging."

She glanced up to see Eric, with Lisa by his side, Cathy, and half the workers standing around the porch and front lawn.

She laughed. "Yes. I will. I'll marry you," Judy cried out.

James stood and took her into his arms. He captured her lips, curling her toes for all to see.

Eric cleared his throat. "Hey, enough of that. We've got work to do."

She looked to Lisa. "Don't worry, honey. I'll get cleaned up. The rest of the day will be all about you." But something inside wouldn't let her release James' hand. Instead, she stood on tiptoes and kissed his cheek.

Lisa looked to Eric then back at her. "Oh, I know I'll have the best day of my life, especially with you walking down the aisle by my side."

"What are you talking about?" Judy scanned their faces, noting each mischievous grin. "You guys are conspiring about something, aren't you? Spill it."

"We're having a double wedding!" Lisa shouted with joy.

"We…I…but it's your day. And I don't have a dress—"

"Taken care of." Cathy unzipped a garment bag revealing the white dress she'd hand beaded with her grandmother for the wedding that never happened over forty years ago.

Judy touched the satin fabric and toyed with the fine beading. "I can't. I mean, it won't even fit."

"Altered to perfection." Cathy beamed.

"You couldn't have done that. How long have you guys known he was going to ask me?"

"I just told Eric and Lisa last night." James stood behind her, holding her shoulders.

"I started the alterations the day after he arrived in town. I had faith you two would figure things out. If not, I was going to tie you two together and say the vows for you." Cathy zipped the bag back up.

Judy looked at Eric. "What about a marriage license?"

James spun her around to face him. "We'll take care of that Monday. For now, I just want to hear you say you want to spend the rest of your life with me in front of God and all our friends." James kissed the top of Judy's head. "Go get ready, my love."

Chapter Twenty-Nine

THE ORGANIST, seated on the raised platform by the house, struck the first notes of the wedding march and all the guests stood and faced the aisle. White ribbons floated off the rows of chairs and a red carpet covered the grass in the front yard. The farmhouse had been transformed into something from an old movie.

James kept his gaze locked on them as Judy and Lisa stepped out onto the front porch. Their beauty awed him, as it did Eric who gasped at his side.

They descended the steps, walking gracefully down the aisle, side by side. Lisa, a young beauty, her dress a perfect design to show off her belly, yet her slender arms and neck were accentuated with her up-do and pearl necklace.

Judy, though, took his breath away, her auburn hair and green eyes bright against the white dress. The intricate pearl detail and lace took him back to another time, one of hope and innocence.

Coming to the end of the aisle, they each took their groom's hand and the four of them stood at the front together.

The preacher held the Bible and said, "Dearly Beloveds and Honored Guests, we are gathered here this day, in the sight of

God and the company assembled, to witness the giving and receiving of the marriage vows. Marriage is an institution ordained of God and is not to be entered into lightly, or in jest, and only after much consideration." Facing the couples, he said, "Do you, Eric Gaylord, and you, James Benjamin, take these women, Lisa Mortan and Judy Gaylord, to be your lawfully wedded wives, to have and to hold, in sickness and in health, in good times and in woe, for richer or poorer, keeping yourself solely unto her for as long as you both shall live? If so, answer *I do*.

James looked into Judy's eyes and with all his will spoke loud enough for all his friends and family in Sweetwater County to hear. "I do."

Eric echoed beside him.

The preacher turned to Lisa and Judy. "Do you, Lisa Mortan and do you, Judy Gaylord, take these men, Eric Gaylord and James Benjamin, to be your lawfully wedded husbands, to have and to hold, in sickness and health, to love, honor, and obey, in good times and in woe, for richer or poorer, keeping yourself solely unto him for as long as you both shall live? If so, answer *I do*."

Judy's chest rose and fell before she answered in unison with Lisa. "I do."

"If there be anyone present who may show just and lawful cause why these couples may not be legally wed, let him speak now or forever hold his peace."

Standing beside Judy, Cathy cleared her throat. "I've got a shotgun in my trunk, people, and I'm not afraid to use it."

The crowd broke into laughter, easing James' nerves a little.

The rest of the ceremony he held tight to Judy's hands and the world disappeared around them.

Then the preacher reached out with his hand. "Rings please."

"We don't—"

"Here." Cathy handed the preacher her wedding ring and her late husband's.

James watched Judy fight the tears filling her eyes as she mouthed *thank you* to Cathy. They exchanged the rings and vowed their love for one another to God.

For the first time since he was sixteen, he felt loved, calm, and happy. And by the way Judy kissed him, he knew she felt the same.

As the preacher announced them an official couple, cheers echoed through the pasture and surrounding woods.

He looked up at the sky.

"She's smiling down on us," Judy whispered.

James nodded. "I know. And scolding me for taking so long."

The crowd continued to applaud as the four of them found their way into the farmhouse.

Judy stopped in the sitting room. "I forgot to tell you, this would make a great wedding venue. But I'm guessing you've changed your mind about selling."

James sighed and watched people milling around out the front window. "Yes. I think this is a home. One I hope to fill with grandkids." He winked at Eric.

Eric smacked his palm to his forehead. "Oh, no. We have two of them now."

Cathy, Marcus, and Rose entered the sitting room.

Rose held tight to Marcus. "That was beautiful. Would you ever think about someone else having a wedding here?"

Eric cleared his throat. "You two have plenty of time and a lot to work out before that happens. Don't forget about our appointment on Thursday."

"I won't," Rose said.

Marcus shook both their hands. "Congratulations. I only hope I get to marry the girl I love someday." He slid a not-so-secret glance at Rose. "Although, I hope it doesn't take us that long."

Cathy smiled and nudged Rose in the side. "It better take a little time though, or your daddy'll have Marcus' head." She scooted around Rose and wrapped her arms around Judy. "Congratulations."

Judy held tight for a moment before releasing her. "Thank you, for everything. You're the best friend a girl could ever have. I love you."

"I love you, too."

Judy turned to James. "I guess there are such things as happy endings after all. You are my happy ending."

James pulled her into his arms. "And you mine."

THE END

Ham Salad Recipe

Ham Salad was a favorite of James when he was dating Judy before he'd left for the war. This recipe is from when Judy had packed a picnic lunch one spring afternoon and met James by the lake.

Ingredients

- 2 cups Ham, chopped
- 2 Hard Boiled Egg, chopped
- ½ cup Celery, finely chopped
- ½ cup Mayonnaise
- 2 Tablespoons Sweet Pickle Relish
- 1 teaspoon Yellow Mustard
- ¼ teaspoon Black Pepper
- ½ teaspoon Sugar, optional, depending on your relish.

Directions:

Chop the ham as finely as desired. Place boiled egg in a medium sized bowl and mash with a fork. Add the chopped ham.

celery, mayonnaise, pickle relish, yellow mustard, sugar, and black pepper. Use a wooden spoon and mix together well. Add more mayo or pickle juice for a creamier ham salad. Season with salt if needed.

Refrigerate for an hour or two before serving.

Readers Guide

1. How would you have reacted to discovering that your first love was alive after decades of believing him dead?

2. Do you believe a love can last through war, time apart, and secrets the way it did for Judy and James?

3. A lifelong friendship can sometimes be complicated, Judy and Cathy are no different. Could you have kept such a big secret from your best friend all those years? Do you think Cathy did it out of love or jealousy?

4. If you were Judy, would you have been able to forgive Cathy for keeping such a huge secret from you all those years?

5. Despite believing James had died, Judy blamed herself for their separation since she'd been with another man after vowing her loyalty to James. Do you think you would've felt the same way?

6. Do you think James's mother hid the documentation in the old

farm house to force him to return after her death in hopes of reuniting him with his true love?

7. Judy made a good point. James could've had someone look for the documentation and send it to him. Do you think he went there in hopes of reuniting with Judy despite his fear?

8. If James had returned years earlier, do you think they could've reconciled then, or do you believe that the years brought wisdom to them both?

9. If James had returned from war without PTSD, and believed he was good for Judy, do you think he would've fought for her then?

10. Who was your favorite character in Spring in Sweetwater County?

SUMMER IN SWEETWATER COUNTY

Marcus Vega and Rose Burton meandered across the swinging bridge hand in hand. The breeze danced through Rose's hair, flipping the long strands into Marcus's face. He tugged her to his side and tucked the stray hair behind her ear. His mouth opened slightly and her skin heated at his closeness.

Leaning in, he brushed his lips across her mouth and whispered, "You're so beautiful. If I were a painter, I'd want you to be my muse."

She giggled. "You don't have to court me, you know. My heart already belongs to you. Although, my mother warned me the day she met you that your suave moves would distract me from things that matter."

Sliding his nose across her cheek, he nipped her earlobe. "And now? Is my suaveness distracting you?"

Her neck fevered at his closeness. She took a long breath, inhaling his scent of fresh honey shampoo and ocean breeze. She rested her head against his chest and took a moment to collect herself. Something she'd struggled to do since the first time Marcus smiled at her a year ago.

Perhaps it was because he was from the wrong side of the

creek and didn't meet her parents' approval. Or maybe it was the two years age difference. No, it was more than that, so much more.

He tipped her head and pressed his lips more firmly to hers. Everything about Marcus Vega sent her senses into a whirlwind.

The bridge swayed. She stumbled, dropping the picnic basket, then clutched his bicep to keep from falling.

"I've gotcha." Marcus cuddled her into his strong embrace, his six-feet-two inches engulfing her small frame in a way that made her feel safe from everything in the world.

She shivered at the thought of him so close. Even now, a year from when they'd met, there was something inexplicable about him. The movement of his hips when he walked, his boyish grin, or perhaps his strong build. Rose wasn't sure, but she believed it was more than that. Despite what her parents thought, his heart was the purist she'd ever known.

"Hey, you're shaking. Let's get you some food, or your parents'll kill me."

Rose shifted away and strung her fingers through his. "They'd kill you anyway if they knew we were alone out here."

Marcus chuckled. "True."

They reached the end of the bridge and she guided him to a clearing on the other side of the trees. She retrieved the blanket and smoothed it over the bright green grass. The hot summer sun was masked by the dense canopy, but still provided plenty of light.

"I'm glad you could take the day off from work so we could talk. I have something I want to tell you."

Marcus retrieved a sandwich and handed it to her. "Eat first. Did you check your blood sugar?"

Rose nodded and sat cross-legged in front of him. "It was fine this morning."

Marcus quirked a brow. "But you were shaking back there."

She felt a blush rush up her neck to her cheeks. "Um, that wasn't from blood sugar."

Marcus chuckled again. "Oh." He cupped her cheek and kissed her forehead. "I'm glad I still have that effect on you."

"Always." She smiled before taking a bite of her ham and cheese, stalling to gather her nerves. Marcus handed her a bottle of water and she sipped, washing down the salty flavor. "Do you remember me mentioning a few months back about speaking to an attorney?"

He lowered his bottle, his gaze narrowing. "Yes, but we agreed—"

"No, you demanded. That's not how this relationship works, mister." She capped her water and set it aside. "Hear me out."

He nodded. "Okay, go ahead. I'm listening."

"You want to go to college and so do I."

He opened his mouth, but she held up her hand to stop him.

"You promised to hear me out. Not a word until I'm done." Rose took a long breath. "I want to go to college and I'll have enough credit hours to graduate high school at the end of summer. I want you to go with me. We'll share an apartment and the expenses."

"You mean your father will pay." Marcus shifted away from her, the way he did when she spoke of her father.

"No. I'm talking about you and me, without my father's money. We'll both work and put ourselves through college. I don't want to work for my father, and I want to go to the college of my choice. It's my life, I should have a say in it."

He picked at a blade of grass that had blown onto the blanket. "Rose, listen. I love you, but you don't know how the real world works. You've been taken care of your entire life. Working full time and going to school is the hard way to go. I promise, I'll wait for you. There's no one I'll ever love more than you." He leaned in, but she refused to let his kisses distract her.

"You sound like my parents. Why does everyone treat me like an invalid? I have diabetes, not cancer."

"Rose Burton, that's not fair. I've never treated you that way.

You're the strongest, most beautiful, intelligent, sexy woman I've ever known, but you can also be the most stubborn. You and your father are more alike than you think."

Anger rolled over her. "Then why did you—"

Marcus grabbed her hand, keeping her from pulling away. "Because I don't want you to suffer." His accent thickened with emotion. "You deserve better."

"Not better than you." She fought the rising fear of losing him.

He kissed each of her knuckles. "Don't worry. I'm powerless to let you go, but not selfish enough to ruin your life before it begins. I had to get my GED instead of finishing high school because I had to start working to support my family after my father's injury. I don't want that for you. I want to give you the world, not heartache. Besides, I can't leave my father."

"Why? You haven't had enough abuse?"

Marcus's hand slid from hers and she cupped her mouth, as if to catch the words. But it was too late.

"I'm sorry. I didn't mean..."

"Yes, you did. I know how everyone sees my old man, but he was once a great father and husband. But his injury and then death of his wife left him no more than a shell."

Rose shuffled closer and tentatively placed a hand on his arm. "I'm sorry, but as much as you want for me, I want that for you as well."

He shifted, spreading his legs apart and he pulled her into him. "Every time I think I should give up on him, I think about how *I* would be if anything happened to you."

Rose struggled for what to say. She didn't want to hurt him, but he deserved a better life. "How long will you give him? Your entire life? Marcus, you'd never turn your back on anyone."

He kissed the top of her head. "We never know what we're capable of until we're faced with a challenge. I turned to drugs when my mother died, too."

She straightened and faced him. "Yes, but you cleaned up on your own. You've got a job now and a sexy girlfriend." She winked.

"True. Perhaps he just needs a little longer."

Sitting on her knees, Rose ran her thumb over the small cleft in his chin. "He has until fall. That's when I'm going to college."

"Rose...you can't."

She leaned back and crossed her arms over her chest. "Wasn't it you that just said I was stubborn. Well, I'm about to show you just how stubborn I am."

About the Author

Ciara Knight is a USA TODAY Bestselling Author, who writes clean and wholesome romance novels set in either modern day small towns or wild historic old west. Born with a huge imagination that usually got her into trouble, Ciara is happy she's found a way to use her powers for good. She loves spending time with her characters and hopes you do, too.

Made in United States
Orlando, FL
30 April 2026

81021163R00099